HAUNTED
BY LEGACY

Editing by Becky Johnson at Hot Tree Editing

Proofreading by Samantha Brennan

Cover design by Dovnik Designs

Title font by Julie Nicholls

ISBN: 978-0-6487871-3-6 (paperback)

ISBN: 978-0-6487871-2-9 (ebook)

ALSO BY SHAY LAURENT

Everleigh Cole Novels
Haunted By Legacy
Burned By Fury

The Shifters & Sorceresses Trilogy
Wolf of Choice

For all the souls that need to escape, if only for a chapter.

CONTENTS

MISSING

PAYING A WITCH TO summon my twin sister, Clara, to my home feels infinitely more reasonable the longer I stare at the shabby wooden door in front of me. If it would even work.

Can you summon a *half* demon?

Let's hope not. I certainly wouldn't want to be dragged to God knows where with my pants around my ankles.

I shake my head, trying to suppress my snort at the thought my inner demonic side fires off. The odds of catching an angel-demon hybrid on the toilet while a witch summoned them would be astronomical.

I take one step closer and begin to feel grumpy all over again. I've avoided this bar since we moved to Australia five years ago—way too many supernaturals in one place for me. I still can't believe Clara works here. If she bothered to join the twenty-first century and get a mobile phone, I could have met her someplace else. But knowing Clara's penchant for revenge, and the fact that she's my only living family, I'm braving the wolves' den over the witch summoning.

She's an eternal pain in the arse.

Unable to disagree, I simply pause and look both ways down the street again. It's completely deserted. The fact that it's 10:00 p.m. on a Friday night, and only ten minutes from Sydney's centre, speaks volumes about the power of whoever set the wards here. The stay-away vibes have the humans keeping their distance better than any other supernatural hub in the city.

I sigh, wishing I didn't need to be here, then roll my shoulders to loosen the tension building between them. The urge to release my wings to help get some relief is unusually hard to control tonight.

Shaking my head in resignation, I approach the building and push the unnaturally heavy door open with a small grunt. The Scandinavian werewolf pack that owns the space spared no effort in decorating. The walls are scattered with caged cabinets displaying the pack's relics, while the furniture is all hand-carved hardwood. Coming inside feels like stepping through a portal to another time and place. A dangerous one.

A pair of guards at the base of the timber stairs observe me—one wears a serious look and the other smirks. Their heavy ancestral cloaks hide their bodies, though I can see from the arms peeking out that their muscles are well-defined. The white fur lining their faces makes the ice blue of their eyes more piercing, and I can see the moment they scent my otherness. They stand a little taller and frowns mar their brows. The one to my left flashes a look towards the bar behind him, then back to me, slight confusion added to his features.

I look over his head and find where his gaze went—Clara. My mouth pulls up on one side, amused and a little surprised he made the connection so quickly. My sister is tall, model thin, and has solid ebony hair down to the top of the black skinny jeans she has on. And if the mage-drawn tattoos and decorative weapons she adorns herself with aren't enough to make someone think twice, her glowing red eyes certainly do the trick. Me, on the other hand? I'm tall and thin, too, but my hair is closer to white, my eyes usually golden, and my clothes—well, it depends on where I'm going. While she screams *dangerous*, my appearance says *safe*. At least to humans.

The closer I get to the bar, the more stares come my way. Noses wrinkle. Laughs turn to frowns. Noise turns to quiet. My insides feel like molten lead and the tension between my shoulder blades has doubled by the time I make it to an empty seat at the end of the bar. I look at Clara and give her a tight smile while she glares at the other customers. Nobody in the supernatural world approves of hybrids. My sister and I are a broken rule that lived to tell the tale. If only our parents had too.

Clearly sick of the staring, Clara slams a hardwood tankard on the bar—a reminder to move on. Most of them return to their conversations, aware that pissing her off might have dire consequences. When she first started working here, there were plenty of stares for her too. From what she'd told me, they'd learned to order their drinks and move on pretty quickly. Her choice to be in the thick of the supes was certainly not the path I chose, but she has a purpose, and getting in her way isn't a smart idea.

The bar seems to be filled with vamps, fae, and a couple of werewolves tonight, though I can smell others in the restaurant behind the wall at my back. Most supes at the bar are leaning on the solid timber bench, nursing Viking horns full of mead, whiskey, and cocktails.

I spend the next few hours listening to conversations at the bar: pack turf wars, vampire social events, fae shenanigans and treachery, but nothing about what I came here to find out. I force air out of my nose, sick of being here and impatient for Clara to have a big enough lull to come and talk to me. When I'm about ready to give up and leave, she finally strides over to me.

Clara leans forward over the bar, and I lean in as well so we can kiss each other's cheeks. As she settles back behind the timber benchtop, her ebony hair comes to rest against it, and her eyes bore into mine.

"Everleigh, what brings you here? You look... concerned?" she offers in a mild, hushed voice.

I nod slightly, looking down the bar at the customers who can hear us if they bother to listen in. Which they likely will. "Yes, it wasn't my first choice, but it's not so easy to get hold of you these days." I give her a loaded look before continuing. "I just wanted to know if you've heard about any humans going missing around the city."

She tilts her head and narrows her eyes slightly. "Of course, they go missing all the time. They do terrible things to each other and themselves. They're fucking monsters."

Sighing, I nod again. "Yes, but I meant, have you heard any talk *here* about humans going missing?"

I try to ignore the tremble of fear that runs through me when I remember the clients I lost back in Paris because of the vicious fae.

Clara stiffens and her fiery eyes darken. "Why do you care? I thought you'd leave such things to the enforcers. Or to me."

"Because some of my psychology clients are missing." At the scrunch of her eyebrows, I add, "You know, at my job as a drug and alcohol psychologist? The people I help?"

She snorts indelicately, pulling the attention of some bar patrons, who quickly turn away at the red flash of her eyes. "Oh, right. I forget you work with the humans. I haven't heard any talk in here. It's probably nothing. Just usual human things. You should stay out of it, Everleigh. Let things run their course like they're meant to. If you want to look into supernatural problems, you could always come and help me."

"Haven't you hunted down enough demons, Clara? Ending more of them isn't going to bring our parents back. Besides, surely your boyfriend isn't okay with you cutting down his brethren?" I grimace, failing as usual to understand how she spends her time hunting demons, while happily dating one at the same time.

Her features harden, letting me know I've poked a sore spot again. "Blake understands, Everleigh. He's helping me get rid of the demons who break the Accords. He has his reasons. Anyway, I need to get back to work. I suppose I can keep an ear out, but I wouldn't expect to hear anything from me."

Clara turns and walks away, back to serve more customers, without another glance in my direction. Lips pursed, I stand from the stool, ready to get out of here and back to my apartment. As I walk towards the exit, I feel more eyes watching than I'm comfortable with, but I'm careful not to hurry my steps. Making the supes think I'm scared or something equally as stupid wouldn't end well for me or them. Avoiding fights is safer, though having them forget I exist is my preference. It's easier to stay around the humans.

Mostly, anyway.

Once outside, the walk through the dark streets back to the train station makes me wish I could release my wings from the ether, spread them, and fly to my apartment. Public transport might be convenient, but late at night, it seems to be filled with unruly humans that I would rather avoid dealing with. Unfortunately, releasing my expansive white wings, with their slight golden glow, would be a violation of the Council's Accords. According to our laws, supes should remain hidden, and anyone who decides to try and out us to the humans would be in for a long and painful death. Since I lost both my parents after they broke Council decrees, sticking to them is an absolute for me. I have no interest in being dragged before the Council. For anything.

As I stand on the train platform, I can't help thinking of my parents. Talking to Clara, seeing all the supes, thinking of my wings—there are too many reasons not to remember them. Estelle, my mother, had wings so much like my own, and I will always remember the way she used to wrap them around me. If I close my eyes, I can almost feel the warmth, her love enveloping me with her wings and arms holding me close. The sweet fragrance of roses. Her gentle face and eyes were always so full of love.

How anyone could consider wiping her from existence has never made sense, and every time I remember she's gone it's like a knife being forced through my heart. My father, Arinthall, was never the same after she was killed. He had loved and cared for us until we were old enough to do it ourselves, but he seemed to revert back to the vengeful demon he was before he met her once she was gone.

The screech of brakes pulls me back to reality as the train rolls into the station. I shake my head, trying to ground myself back into the present, letting my parents slide back into my memories. Wistfulness and sadness fill me as I step onto the train and take a seat. I don't bother to try to get comfortable since I'll get off shortly.

On Monday morning, after a weekend of no news of my missing clients, I walk into my workplace in one of the tall buildings in Darling Harbor. Once I reach my office, I take in the views from the one-way floor-to-ceiling glass windows on the fifteenth floor. The water is choppier than usual despite the hot, clear summer day, almost like a bad omen. I sigh, annoyance taking over at what feels like my powers deciding, perhaps, they have something to say, but they can't quite be sure.

I hear the elevator ding in the distance and smile, knowing my best friend, Henry, must be here since no one else is ever in this early. I know we aren't meant to get close to humans, but I need some kind of support doing a job like this, and it's not like Clara is willing to talk to me about human problems. Maybe one day the Council will agree with the growing faction of supporters wanting us to reveal ourselves, and then it won't be such a big deal. Until then, I make sure to keep things strictly human around Henry.

Outside my office is a small waiting room partitioned from others, and I wander through it and out to the main reception. After following the corridor around to the right, I go through Henry's waiting area and head straight into his office. He looks up, his olive skin glowing from the rays of sun streaming in his windows, the smile on his face as bright as always.

"Ev, you look lovely. How are you?" he asks.

"I'm all right, Henry. I see you tried something new for casual Mondays."

Henry grins, pulling on the suspenders he wears attached to his pale beige pants every day without fail, looking like he's walked out of a different time. "You know me. Can't leave the house without 'em. My pants would fall down otherwise."

I laugh at his saucy smirk and the wink he offers me. His pants couldn't fall down if they tried. They fit perfectly on his tall, lean, muscled frame. Henry always makes me laugh. There's something about him that just draws people in and I'm sure it helps with his clients.

After rearranging a few papers on his desk, Henry looks back up at me, lounging against his doorframe. "Lunch today? I was thinking Italian. I've got a hankering for some *boscaiola*."

"That sounds delicious, but I'll let you know a little later. I think my books are pretty full." I glance down at the old-fashioned watch on my wrist and stand up. "Speaking of, I need to get back to my room and prep some stuff for my first appointment. Chat soon, yeah?"

"For sure," he says, smiling and returning my wave as I head out the door and back to my office.

I immediately get to work and time flies. When 11:00 a.m. rolls around, I stretch and go to the door to invite Sophie in, wondering what style she will have her auburn curls in today. When I see the waiting room is empty, I wander back to my desk and recheck my calendar. I'm sure I haven't misread it—I'd think after 137 years that wouldn't happen, but it still does now and again.

Nope. She should be here. What in the hellish realms is going on with my damn clients?

An emergency contact call later I discover that Sophie might have been client zero, since she hasn't been seen in just over three weeks. That's longer than my other missing clients.

If this is more fae savagery, someone is going to pay.

I make a few calls to recheck some details of my other missing clients and where they were last seen while trying to push down the bile rising in my throat. They'd all been seen at the community kitchen down by the harbor on the days they went missing. I make a note in Sophie's file that she is a no-show again, feeling the increasing pressure to figure out what is going on. Once a client misses three sessions, if we can't make contact, we have to file a missing person's report with the police. That's today for Sophie.

My angelic intuition is telling me that something supernatural is going on, but I haven't found any evidence to support it yet. I know the Council prefers supernatural problems to be managed by the enforcers rather than the human police, but getting them involved would draw unnecessary attention to me if I am wrong.

I need more information.

As I grab my keys, I say a half-hearted prayer that this is just "a human problem," as Clara suggested, and not a supernatural one like my gut is telling me. Though considering I'm half demon, I doubt the big guy is listening anyway.

I check my watch; it's time to get going as the community kitchen will have started serving customers by now. If I can't find any evidence of supernatural involvement by this afternoon, I'll put in the missing person's report for Sophie.

In my rush to get down to the harbor, I walk out the door and nearly collide with my best friend. "Oh, sorry, Henry! Is everything okay?"

"Woah. Are you all right, Ev? I just came to check in about lunch."

Ahh shitballs.

"Ah, right, I forgot. Sorry, Henry, something's come up and I need to step out. Rain check?"

Henry's brow furrows and concern is clear on his features. "Sure, but you look worried. Anything I can help you with?"

Indecision wars within me. I don't really want Henry around anything supernatural, but he knows these clients too. All of those missing are in our fortnightly group therapy class, so if it is just a human problem, he would probably want to know. Then again, I don't want him to get into trouble at work either.

I've taken too long to answer, and Henry lifts his hand and rests it on my shoulder, giving me a reassuring squeeze. "You know I'm here to help, right, Ev? What's going on?"

I suck in a breath and let it out slowly, taking what feels like the biggest risk since my parents were killed. "You know the clients from our evening group?" At his nod, I continue, "Well, some of the ones who didn't attend our last session are also missing from individual sessions. I'm just"—I drop my voice, not wanting anyone in the office to overhear— "going to pop down to where they were last seen and ask around."

Henry's concern seems to morph into something deeper. "Two of my clients from that group haven't shown this week either. They're pretty inconsistent with individual sessions, so I didn't think much of it. I didn't realize there were others. What's going on?"

"I don't know, and I know it's outside our job description, but I'm just going to ask around at the community kitchen where they were last seen. Maybe somebody there knows something. If I don't hear anything, I'll need to put a report in for Sophie today."

He nods, a look of resolution taking over his features. "I'm coming."

Conflicted, but knowing I can't take it back, I nod. "Let's just make it quick, ask around during our lunch hour, and come back in time for our next clients."

He grimaces, then steps back and gestures for me to lead the way.

As we walk out the door and into the street, the sweltering midday sun engulfs my entire body. While my hybrid status means I'm not as affected by the elements as much as humans, the heat here is enough to dry me out and build up a little sweat. The silence as we walk feels less companionable than usual. Maybe because, despite not having a shred of evidence, I can't stop the terrible scenarios running through my head—an unlikely group relapse sadly being on the lower end of the "oh shit" scale.

Fae might be poisoning our clients, like they did to mine in Paris fifty years ago, driving them to paranoia, making them dangerous to themselves and others. Or maybe werewolves kidnapped them for their hunting games for the next full moon. Hells, demons could be torturing them while we walk down the path by the water to try and find them. Angels typically stay out of trivial things like this, but with the growing tide of unrest between and within supes, nothing would surprise me at this point.

When a long breath escapes me, Henry gently bumps into my shoulder and offers me a small, reassuring smile. If only life were as simple as he believes it to be.

The community kitchen is just as I remember. A van is set up by some office buildings, and people are spread out eating from paper plates between the van and the harbor. The cool breeze coming off the water offers all the customers a little relief from the stifling heat.

"How about you chat with some of the people eating over by the water while I go and chat to the ladies serving the food?" I say. At his reluctant look, I offer a wry smile and add, "We don't want to be late back to the office."

Henry nods and walks away with a thumb hooked around one of his suspender straps—a nervous habit.

After fifteen minutes of speaking with the women serving the food, and the customers getting their lunch, I've learned nothing helpful. I make my way over to Henry hoping he's had more luck than me.

"Any news?" I ask.

"A couple of the teenagers over near the water said they haven't seen Sophie, but they saw Andrea, from our Tuesday group, walk off on her own two nights ago after dinner. They said it was pretty late and she seemed kind of agitated, and that she'd been muttering something about being watched." He points to a gap between a few buildings closer to an industrial complex. "They said she went off through the alley, but they haven't seen her since—figured she was lying low. The girls said it didn't look like Andrea was on anything, but do you think maybe she was?"

Shit. What am I supposed to say to that? It's the logical human explanation, but my gut tells me it's not right, and I hate lying outright. Especially to Henry. And offering him what might be the truth would land both of us in an early grave. I already risked enough telling him I was worried when my intuition was firing off.

I try to smooth out the frown I feel marring my forehead and swallow the burning feeling in my throat before I offer an unlikely half-truth. "I'm not sure, Henry. I suppose she could be. Look, we've asked all we can. Why don't you head over and order us some pasta and I'll meet you there? I just want to check one more thing."

"Honestly, I'd rather stick with you, Ev. If something hinky is going on here, then the two of us staying together is better than you going on your own." He pauses briefly, and hesitantly adds, "Though, we *could* just call the police now?" His questioning tone leaves me feeling a very human amount of guilt and doubt over trying to investigate things myself.

I guess to a human, calling the police seems like the logical choice. Hells, even to a supernatural it would seem fine... to most of us anyway. Since there are plenty of witches and mages monitoring human events, we almost always end up with someone on the scene who can cover up the evidence. Plenty of hackers and higher-ups who could change the findings. But because of how much I'm hated, calling the Council enforcers could end in me being iced out, and my clients mean too much for me to take that road if I can avoid it. Sure, I could lodge a form at the Council of the Accord office. Maybe I'd even learn the truth in another fifty years or so. But my missing clients' families deserve better than the "forever missing" status they would get if the enforcers were involved. I owe it to them to check it out first.

Rolling my shoulders back and down, wishing pointlessly yet again that I could release my wings, I try to reassure Henry. "I'll give them a call when I get back to the office, okay? I just want to follow up on what the teenagers said. I'm okay if you just order lunch and I meet you there."

In fact, it's probably ideal.

Just take the damn hint!

He stands a little taller, bunching his shoulders up and puffing his chest a little, and I sigh internally, knowing I'll be safer on my own but resigning myself to the consequences of including him in the first place. I nod, then head off along the wharf, trying to keep grounded by focusing on the feel of the sea breeze touching the small hairs on the back of my neck.

When we reach the entrance to the alley, the noise and stench are overwhelming. The air-conditioning generators running in the alley, paired with the boat horns from the harbor, leave me barely able to hear myself think. It reeks of rot, but it's so potent, it's hard to tell whether it's human or animal or moldy food. Henry's wrinkled nose and the arm he's using to cover it tell me it must be almost as bad for him. Almost. This is one of those times I wish I had better control over my supernatural senses.

Further down the alley, rubbish is strewn everywhere. Bags look to have been torn from the dumpsters before being searched and discarded, and bits of food, empty bottles, and other indistinguishable, filthy scraps lay haphazardly on the ground. I do my best to walk over the mess without stepping in anything that might make me lose the sugar cookie I ate earlier. At a tug on my sleeve, I see Henry pointing to an unhoused person's shelter a little ahead, and a heaviness adds to the ache in my chest as I think about how desperate someone would need to be to reside in this alleyway.

Henry steps ahead of me and leans in to open the tent. Within a second, he stumbles back, his skin the color of a hospital sheet, his mouth slightly askew. My stomach feels queasy as I step around him to get a better look. A pair of sneakers attached to someone's legs hang awkwardly through the flap, both at an unnatural angle. Another step shows a dried smear of blood. As soon as I see it, it's like my nose homes in on the scent, blocking out everything else from the alley.

The strength of the iron-like smell is overwhelming, and I close my eyes briefly, bracing myself for the worst.

TROUBLE

IT'S CARNAGE. IT TAKES me a moment to locate the faces within the gore. The attacker's lack of control suggests a freshly turned vampire is responsible.

Anguish pulses through my chest when I recognize two of my clients. Michael has been thrown down on his side, his legs snapped near the knees. It's his feet poking out of the entrance. Terror and pain cover his pale face, telling me he was alive for at least some of this torture. His throat has been completely ripped out and pieces of sinew hang free. My stomach turns when I see parts of his spine have been sucked clean while others were gnawed on.

Andrea lays crumpled like a broken doll, thrown in on top of Michael. The baby vamp was clearly getting full, because while one side of her neck is missing, the other just has fang marks—they're less crazed when they aren't so thirsty.

The angelic side of me feels a deep, sad ache at the senseless loss of these two beautiful souls, both utterly kind despite their tragic pasts, but my demonic side is furious.

Finding and killing this fucker is a must.

The sound of vomit has me spinning to look at Henry, and I curse under my breath. I'd been too distracted to think about what this might mean for him.

What in the hells was I thinking, letting him come here?

Henry looks up at me, face pale and drawn, bits of vomit sticking to his chin. He opens and closes his mouth several times, but no words come out. I move closer and put an arm around him, trying to rub gentle circles on his back as I fret over just what details he noticed, but trying to reassure him anyway. "It'll be okay, Henry."

After leading him a little away from the tent and a few minutes have passed by, I hear Henry trying to form words. I lean closer, fear of the consequences of him seeing something he shouldn't have squeezing my chest like a vise.

"Were th-th-those f-f-fang marks?"

I close my eyes for a moment, not knowing a curse word bad enough to cover this situation. When I open them, Henry is staring into my eyes. At this point, I'm not sure that muddying the truth is even an option. The marks were obvious, and somebody's Master has some questions to answer—baby vamps aren't supposed to be just made and set free.

Is this carnage another message for me, just like in Paris?

As I open my mouth to try and give Henry a simple kind of truth, movement comes from the same entry to the alleyway as the one we'd used. My gaze shoots in that direction, and my nose catches the scent of a wolf before my eyes see it.

Fantastic.

The wolf, in its human form, walks into view. His muscled but lithe physique seems to magically avoid the garbage scattered beneath him and his eyes pierce mine immediately. The blueish-gray is so dark, it looks like it belongs to the depths of the ocean. Despite the fact he looks good enough to eat, I can't help but groan, because I know this werewolf. When he's close enough to speak, he stops.

"Why is there a human here?" Alaric asks, deadpan.

Hmph. Hello to you too, wolf.

Henry freezes for a second, somehow seeming to lose more color, before hooking an arm around mine and finding the courage to stand up straighter. I feel conflicted. His protective instinct is sweet, but things have just become unbelievably worse, and the more Henry says, the harder it will be to get us out of this. I grab his arm and squeeze it, trying to give him a warning glance, but he only has eyes for Alaric.

"What do you mean, human?" Henry demands. "And what the heck are you doing here? Did you do this?"

Alaric follows Henry's hand as he waves towards our broken, mangled clients, then looks back and arches one white-blond brow at me as he purses his lips, clearly displeased.

"He's here with me," I offer, trying to give as little away as I can.

"You know that is against the rules, Miss Cole. Surely, keeping to the Accords is your highest priority."

Henry's head whips around to me. "You know this guy?"

I look at Henry and see a mix of shock tinged with suspicion in both his eyes and his aura. I offer him a small nod but can't give him much in the way of reassurance. I turn back to Alaric and try to think of the best way out of this. "I know the rules, *Mr. Bane*. This wasn't exactly planned."

"You're saying you both wandered down this alley and happened to come across these people who you then killed?"

I talk over Henry's spluttering, completely unimpressed with Alaric's assessment. "I had nothing to do with killing *my clients*, Alaric. If you take a look, I'm sure you will determine the cause of death yourself quite quickly." I gesture to myself. "It's clearly not something we could have done."

I step back away from my clients, taking Henry with me, then gesture for Alaric to take a look himself.

He stares at me with an inscrutable expression for a moment longer, long enough that I wish I could read the aura of other supernaturals as easily as humans. I watch as he goes to the small tent and pulls back the flap. A low rumble seems to emit from his chest, and I shiver, unable to stop myself. Henry, on the other hand, seems to quiver and tries to pull me further away from Alaric and the tent. I offer him a small, reassuring smile but look back at what's happening.

Alaric's gaze is livid. If steam could pour from his ears, it appears it may just do that. "Who did this?"

"I have no idea. We got here not long before you did. How did you even know to come here?"

Alaric shifts his weight from one foot to another but doesn't answer my question.

I snort inelegantly. "Fine." Then I turn to Henry, "We need to go now. Come on."

At the same time, Henry says, "We need to call someone."

Alaric moves to stand directly in our path and says, "You're not going anywhere."

I rub my temples. "Henry, Alaric will take care of it. He works... for the police."

Alaric steps close enough that the warmth radiating from his wolf feels akin to being burned in the sweltering heat of the summer sun. "Neither of you are going anywhere. I have questions, and he needs to be... taken care of."

My muscles tighten as I take a step closer to Alaric and lower my voice to an almost whisper that I know he will hear but Henry won't. I focus hard on trying to hide the violent red that's threatening to take over my eyes. "We *are* leaving. We didn't do anything wrong here, and he doesn't understand anything." Reluctantly, I add, "I can come and find you later or go to the Accords office."

He shakes his head in return, two sharp movements left and right.

A huff of air escapes my nose. I know Henry being here is bad, but he doesn't really understand what is happening, and

I'm sure I can explain things away. And I don't want another important person in my life to lose theirs.

"He doesn't understand," I repeat with a quiet, tightly controlled voice. "Just let him go."

Before he can respond, a quiet but high-pitched sound comes from the other end of the alley. Something rolling. I step back and turn to see two women walking towards us, each pulling a wheeled paramedic's gurney behind them. Their muted auras tell me they're likely witches—more human than supernatural, at least to my senses—and I move slightly so I stand between them and Henry. The last thing I need is Henry being killed before I can contest Alaric's decision with the Council.

My heart starts racing when a tingle runs over my skin, alerting me to magic being cast by the witches. If I focus, I can see a projection of their muted auras pushing out in front of them, but thankfully, all they are doing is clearing the way through the debris. Behind me, I hear Henry suck in a sharp breath that gets stuck, causing him to cough and splutter. Guilt and worry for my friend wash through me. Every second we spend in this alley is making things so much worse, and I hope he can keep it together long enough for me to get him out of this.

Alaric waves the witches over to the tent. They're both dressed in one-piece black coveralls that look like nothing would stick to them. The one closest has hair so dark it seems to absorb the low light in the alley, while her partner has vibrant red hair and piercing blue eyes. I'm grateful when they pay little attention to Henry and me, instead focusing on getting to Alaric and the bodies.

When they get close enough to peer into the tent, the one with the dark hair hisses, sounding disgusted. "Fucking vamps," she mutters, hopefully too quietly for Henry to hear, then climbs straight in and starts collecting the first body, calling her partner in to help after a moment.

I turn to check on Henry, and I'm relieved to see he has a little more color than he did before. He locks his gaze with mine, and I prepare for questions I don't really want to answer.

I look at the bodies of my clients and feel ill.

"It's not your fault, Ev. Everything will be all right."

I sure hope it's not my fault, but it wouldn't be the first time people's lives were ruined because of me and my family.

I shake my head slightly to clear the unhelpful thoughts and offer him a small smile. "Thanks, Henry."

Alaric simultaneously bursts into our conversation and our personal space. "That remains to be seen. What are you both doing here?"

I turn and glare at Alaric, resigned to more questioning but not liking it at all. "Some of my clients have gone missing. Henry's too. We were just following up with the people who saw some of them last. They told us this was the way they went home several nights ago. We came to check it out."

He offers me a glare in return. "And after the last incident, you thought that bringing the human with you was the right way to do things."

I grind my teeth, refusing to bite, hating the fact that he always seems to know exactly where to poke to make it hurt. "I had no solid proof of what was going on here." Trying to be purposefully vague for Henry's sake. "Maybe if you were doing your job well enough, we wouldn't have walked in on this anyway."

A low, warning growl slips from Alaric, and I try to hold in a petty grin.

One point to me.

"What else do you know about this?" he asks, a slight growl to his words.

"Like I said, some of our clients have gone missing. Another three, at least. I don't know if it's related." Focusing back on my clients instead of antagonizing Alaric brings the heaviness in my chest back to the front of my mind, and I do my best not to let it show.

A look of contemplation crosses Alaric's face. "There have been six other bodies collected over the last few weeks. You need to come and see if you can identify them."

The heaviness inside me turns sharp once more, and the guilt that this is probably my fault begins to take over. Henry's touch on my hand reminds me he is still here and that I need to get him out.

"Fine," I say to Alaric. "But I'm taking Henry back to work first."

He shakes his head. "You know he isn't going anywhere."

The finality of the sentence makes me wonder if he's going to try and kill Henry right here in the alley so the witches can drag his body off on their gurneys too.

"He's leaving, Alaric. We're both due back at work"—I glance at my watch— "in about ten minutes."

He looks pointedly at the tent, then back at me, and a chill seeps into me. "People go missing all the time, Miss Cole. You are, of course, free to return to work, but you will need to go to the Council building this evening to see if any of your other clients are there."

His careless use of words is causing a fire to build in me as he makes it harder for me to explain this away to Henry.

Before I can open my mouth, Henry taps my shoulder. He's standing tall, trying to appear brave. "I don't know how you know this guy, Ev, but clearly, he's bad news. He's not acting like any cop I've ever seen. Just go, Ev, while you still can."

"Yes, *Ev*, listen to the human. Just go."

"Don't call me that, Alaric. It's reserved for my friends." I turn back to Henry and grab his hand. "You don't understand what you're asking me to do. I'm not going to desert you."

There is no way Alaric is letting him walk away. I guess it's all in for Henry now—or death.

My gaze whips back to Alaric and I take a deep breath, trying to build my resolve for what I need to do next and what it's going to cost me. "There's been enough bloodshed already. I invoke the Raphilian Rite. Get me a meeting with the Council of the Accord."

I sit close to Henry in the back of the witches' van with the bodies of our clients laying at our feet, silently cursing Alaric for being such an ass. He knew he had no choice but to let me take Henry before the Council, but it didn't mean he had to be nice about it. Though, I suppose, maybe he just didn't trust me not to take Henry and run when I said we could make our own way there.

I turn to look at Henry. His eyes seem glued to the sheets over Michael's and Andreas's bodies but his gaze is far away. I gently place a hand on his arm and his forearm tenses beneath me.

"Henry, I'm sorry I've dragged you into all of this. I promise I will do everything I can to get you out safely," I murmur, trying to keep the building fear from my voice and avoid being overheard by the witches in the front seat. "I know you're going to need an explanation, but we don't have time right now. Things are going to seem pretty crazy for a hot minute... like vampires-and-stuff kind of crazy."

Henry's brow furrows. "I don't really get what's going on, but I can see I've stepped right into the middle of something dangerous. I know you'll do everything you can, Ev, of course. Nothing seems believable right now, and I just.... Don't do anything rash, okay? You're important here too."

He's taking this better than any human who has been introduced to our world that I have met. Hopefully it will help in the Council meeting.

I put my left arm around Henry's back and lean into his warmth, easing the slight tremble emanating from his body, grateful all over again for the friend I managed to find in this city, human or not.

"I'll do my best, okay. When we go in here, though, I need you to promise me you'll talk as little as possible. Let me handle things. I'll explain what I can later, when you're hopefully out of danger."

The van screeches to a stop and the back door flies open, and Alaric is looking at us expectantly. I turn to Henry and murmur, "I promise I will explain all of this."

I offer a small, hopeful prayer for my clients as I leave the van. The big guy should at least listen for Andrea and Michael, if not for me.

Henry looks at me, confusion marring his features. I look past him and across the street to follow Alaric's movement and see the problem. To Henry, it looks as though we are standing in front of what appears to be a tall crumbling building, one not even safe enough for the unhoused folk to venture into. Not that the wards would let them pass if they got close enough anyway.

"It's okay. You'll see in a moment. It isn't what you think." I take his hand and lead him gently over to the ward, knowing the only way he can pass through is while having direct contact with a supe who has the intention to take him through. The moment Alaric passes the ward, Henry jerks to a halt.

"Where did he—"

"It's safe," I reassure him. "He's fine. Let's keep going."

The moment we cross the ward, Henry gasps. His features transform to show his awe. What was a crumbling form is now a thirty-story office building with sleek, reflective glass from top to bottom. The wavy-looking façade that spans almost the entire block looks like it belongs with high-end hotels rather than this street of old buildings just outside of the city.

Two shifters in their bear forms stand guard at the main door, and Alaric walks straight inside without pausing to look back at us. I glance at Henry from the corner of my eye and notice he's standing taller, his chest puffed out once more. Judging by the slight gray color of his aura, he's trying to put on a brave face after watching Alaric waltz right in.

I smile a little, despite the dire situation and my growing guilt and fear, grateful again that I have such a good friend in Henry. We make it past the bears with little more than a snort from one of them. Inside, the Council of the Accord building is neutral territory, which means members from all supernatural races can enter, and no singular faction is in charge. The Council of the Accord has a building in most major cities in the world, but the Council members rotate to a new city every twenty-five years. If

I'd known they were moving to Sydney a few years after I did, I would have chosen somewhere else to live.

We walk through the foyer decorated with neutral tones to the reception desk where Alaric is waiting. He points to a form on the table. "You both need to fill this in. I've notified the receptionist to call the Council members, but while you wait, we can go to the morgue."

I nod, lips pursed, and pick up the pen and pass it to Henry. I watch as he fills in his details, thankfully on a blank form, before passing the pen to me. I fill in all my details, reluctantly adding my species, before placing the pen back on the desk. The attendant takes the form to the computer and begins typing. After a few moments, her eyes flick up to me and then back down to continue typing. After several minutes, she hands an identification lanyard to Henry and me, then nods at Alaric.

"Right, this way," he says to us brusquely and heads off to a long hall behind the reception desk. I follow at Henry's pace, letting Alaric get ahead. When he reaches the lift, he leans against the wall and watches us, impatience and something else I can't quite figure out lining his face. When we get close enough, he pokes the Down button, and the heaviness in my chest from earlier returns with force. I falter briefly before continuing towards the elevator, which dings open right in time for us all to walk in.

Alaric's brows furrow as he watches me enter, but I don't have the energy to say anything snarky to him. As we go down the three floors, dread pools within me and I almost drag my feet as we head towards the morgue.

When we reach the door, I turn to Henry. "Would you like to just wait out here? It's likely as bad as what we saw in the alley."

Henry still looks somewhat pale and more than a little conflicted. I grasp the side of his shoulder and squeeze gently. "Just stay here, okay? This has been a rough day already and it's far from done."

He seems to think for a moment longer, staring into my eyes, and eventually nods. His face is a picture of reluctance and relief, and I force my lips into a brief smile before turning to follow Alaric into the artificially cooled room. Thankfully, he opted to stay silent and didn't force the issue.

Once the door clicks shut behind us, Alaric clears his throat quietly. I turn and face him and find him looking more serious. "For what it's worth, Everleigh, I wish you didn't need to do this. This case has been a mess and so are the victims." He huffs out a breath. "I really hope I can solve this soon. Let's make this quick."

Taken aback at how forthcoming and considerate he's being, I nod. The case must be getting to him if he's losing his sharp tone with me so quickly.

He stares a moment longer before walking to the first drawer and turning the large handle. A burst of frosty air floats out as the seal breaks, and Alaric rolls out the cloth-covered table. I can already tell the first body is misshapen, though thankfully the sheet has remained white; the blood, if there was any left, has dried.

Alaric looks at me for confirmation and I nod reluctantly, readying myself to see another client when he lifts the sheet. The first is thankfully not someone I know, and I shake my head, a little relieved. We follow the same routine for the rest of the bodies, and I identify three of them.

I swallow down the lump in my throat before talking. "There's still one of our clients unaccounted for. Sophie. I don't know of anyone else missing," I offer quietly.

He dips his chin and slides the final drawer away before sealing it in. "Got it, thank you. Let's head back up and check on what is happening with the Council."

I draw in a deep breath and brace myself for what comes next. Being involved with supes is far from the top of my desired activities list. Being stuck in a room with the head of every major species while I ask them for a favor... well, I just hope Henry and I make it out of the meeting alive.

CHANGE

HENRY, ALARIC, AND I sit silently outside the penthouse office suite watched by two mages armed to the teeth with weapons and vials of potions. Their loaded coats make them look bulky, and their keen, watchful eyes keep me on alert.

Alaric breaks the silence after looking at his phone. "The Council members are entering through the private elevator. You'll both be called in soon."

"Thank you," I murmur, reluctant to draw the attention of the guards.

Thanks for bloody nothing more like.

Henry says nothing; he's simply sitting, staring into space. When I told him three more of our clients were in the morgue, he'd asked if the same thing had happened to them. Since then, only silence. I really hope he can manage to keep things together to get through this meeting.

A gruff voice from outside the doors startles me from my thoughts. "You three. Inside. Now."

Before I can open my mouth, Alaric bites out, "What do you mean all three of us?"

The mage looks as though he isn't going to answer for a moment, but then scrunches his nose and rubs his head—someone must be talking with him telepathically, and he clearly doesn't like it. "They want an update on the case," he says to Alaric, somewhat less gruffly.

I watch as Alaric's face shuts down. The small amounts of softness, exhaustion, and vulnerability he's shown me are gone, and his stoic expression is back. Showing those same emotions to the Council would be a mistake since they rarely forgive such "weakness."

"Henry, are you ready?" I ask, waiting for him to get up. When he looks at me, I try to control the overwhelming guilt pressing on my chest and offer him a reminder. "You need to have it together in there, okay? Try to look confident even if you don't feel it. And let me do most of the talking."

He staggers slowly to his feet and takes a breath that must fill his lungs to capacity, holds it in for a moment, and then breathes it out completely. He squeezes his eyes shut, stands up taller, then looks at me and nods. "Okay. Let's go."

I offer him what I hope is a reassuring smile and nod, but my insides are writhing with guilt and fear for him.

Alaric walks in first, then steps to the side. The large suite has carpet that appears as soft as a cloud in a blue so deep it looks like the midnight sky. Seven high-end leather chairs with small hardwood side tables are placed in a semi-circle around the room.

A lithe fae female stands at the fore of the chairs and waits for us to file in. Once we are all inside, she speaks. "The Council of the Accord recognizes that you, Everleigh Cole, have invoked the Raphilian Rite, which grants you this audience. The Council reminds you that payment for invocation requires one hundred years of fealty to the angel Raphael, or less if he should consider the debt repaid."

At the mention of one hundred years, Henry looks as though he's about to speak out. I reach out and touch his arm and shake my head once, sharply. Now is not the time.

I look back to the fae female and nod. "I accept."

She lowers her head in acknowledgment and steps to the side. She gestures to the first chair. "Iridessa, queen to the fae."

Iridessa sits regally in her chair, with one ankle tucked behind the other. Her hair is a red so dark it looks as though it is made of rubies spun into fine strands. Her smile appears to hold a thousand secrets, ones some people would kill to possess and, which she would be only too happy to share for the right price. She appears young, only eighteen or so in human years, but I know she is one of the most ancient in the room. Her flowing white gown sparkles despite the low light, as if it glows from the inside out.

Henry's eyes look like they're going to bulge out of his head, and I feel a twinge of guilt that I didn't have more time to explain things to him. We bow our heads and I nudge Henry so he will do the same. Uncertain and shocked, he manages to follow our lead.

The fae moves to gesture to the next chair. "Conall Wiven, king to werewolves and shifters."

The werewolf and shifter king lounges back in his chair, jeans and a loose-fitting shirt covering his clearly muscled physique. Despite the casualness of his outfit, he looks as though he's been chiseled from marble. His ice-blue eyes are piercing, holding mine steadily until he turns to look at Alaric.

Alaric closes his right hand into a fist and places it over his heart before giving his king a low bow from the waist. The lowest bow is always reserved for those you owe fealty to. For me, before today, I would not have offered that bow to anyone. I lower my head in respect to the werewolf and shifter king. Henry follows suit, and the greetings continue.

"Octavia Witt, High Witch," offers the fae.

"Miss Cole. Welcome."

I nod gratefully, sensing a potential ally, though why is unclear. "Miss Witt."

She returns a small smile from light pink lips only a few shades darker than her pale skin. When she sits forward in her chair, her deep violet coat shifts to accommodate her movement. The look on her face seems to convey words unsaid, and I have to refrain from arching my eyebrows in question—if she wants to speak, she will. After another silent moment, a black cat with panther-like features jumps on her shoulder from the back of her chair. When she sits back, we offer bows and wait for the next introduction.

"Solomon Trite, Arch Mage." The fae gestures to the mage without looking in his direction, a pinched expression on her otherwise neutral face. *Curious.*

The mage sits in a cerulean and gold cloak that points out over his shoulders and is held together with what appears to be a solid gold talisman. The center of the talisman glows a fluorescent shade of blue interspersed with writhing black lines. When he doesn't speak, we bow our heads, and then look away.

The fae keeps her distance but does look at the next male in the group as she gestures to him. "Nicon, Ruler of Demons," she says.

Nicon leans forward in his chair, curiosity plain on his face. "Everleigh, daughter of Arinthall, greetings."

Such curiosity is rare to see so openly displayed, though the demon in his black designer suit doesn't seem to care. His red eyes feel as though they call to mine, and I sense the color flicker in my own before I lock it down.

Bloody fiend!

Nicon's small, mischievous grin tells me he got the reaction he wanted, though why he wanted it in this room makes me suspicious.

"Greetings, Nicon, son of Lucifer and Eisheth."

His smile lessens and he offers a small head bow of his own. My heart races as I consider that perhaps the information isn't widely known.

In the next chair sits Raphael, the Archangel. And though I certainly don't need the introduction, it's given anyway. Then it's my turn to offer a deep bow. It feels... unnatural. Stiff. When I stand and look at Raphael, I notice Henry stumble beside me before clutching my arm, his mouth open in a small *O* shape. I realize as soon as he steps closer, and by the golden light reflecting on his skin, that my eyes are glowing. I grimace and turn back to Raphael to see his eyes are glowing in return, the same golden hue as mine and my mother's.

Everyone in the room seems to be holding their breath. I'm sure I could hear a feather hit the ground if one should suddenly fall from a wing. It's normal for an angel's glow to be drawn out by an archangel, but Raphael's eyes should certainly not have glowed in response to mine. After a pregnant pause while Raphael's eyes fade back to their usual blue-gray, he nods to me. "Well met, Everleigh, daughter of Estelle."

I open my mouth to speak, but my heart and mind race so fast that I struggle to put together a response. Why did Raphael's eyes glow like that? The scuff of a boot draws my attention back to the room, and I manage to pull myself together, grateful to whoever had caused the distraction.

"Well met, Archangel Raphael." I bow again, then stand and look at the fae, ready to get the last introduction over with before anything else goes pear-shaped.

When she doesn't move fast enough, Alaric clears his throat, and I catch his glare at the edge of my vision. The fae hurries to make the last introduction, presumably because she's been called out in front of the Council. "This is Orpheus Kildare, the Vampire King."

Henry pales beside me at the introduction, clearly making a connection to what happened in the alley. Thankfully, he still manages to bow with us. When my eyes meet the Vampire King's, I can't help but stare. His inky hair seems to draw color and light from the space around him, and his black clothes blend into his dark skin. The silver of his eyes is like a splash of color in the middle of a lightless night. My gaze is somehow drawn back to his, even though the feeling in my gut is telling me to look away.

I feel like I'm falling into the light. Unable to stop myself. Unwilling to let it end.

Hands touch my left arm, but they feel like phantom hands—not really there. I hear a muffled shout.

Then nothing.

I blink slowly, dashes of color and sound breaking through the haze clouding my mind. After a few seconds, I see Henry and

Alaric leaning over me. Henry is a picture of concern, while Alaric appears simultaneously concerned and exasperated. I groan a little and begin to sit up. When the men help me to my feet, silence falls in the room around us, though as I see the Council members' faces, they all portray varying shades of agitation over whatever just happened. I get the impression they aren't going to address it, either, and considering why I'm here, I reluctantly resign myself to letting it go for now too.

Octavia clears her throat. "We will give you a moment, Miss Cole." She turns her focus on Alaric. "Perhaps you can give us an update on the case in the interim."

"Of course," he says. "So far there have been eight confirmed deaths. All human. All appear to have been killed by a newly turned vampire." He glances briefly at the Vampire King, who makes no acknowledgment of the claim. "Miss Cole and her associate know five of the victims, and confirmed they know of at least one other missing human, all as clients from their place of employment. Three of the victims are unknown. There are no other leads at this point."

He sounds pretty pissed about the lack of progress he's been able to make so far.

Octavia turns to Orpheus. "Do you know anything of this newly turned vampire?"

A purse of his lips is the only displeasure he expresses. "No. I will make inquiries. We all know the change process is highly regulated. This should not have happened."

You don't say. Clearly you need to do a better job.

The Council members nod at Orpheus in acknowledgment of his statement. With that conversation seemingly finished, it means it's back to me now.

Raphael addresses me directly. "Everleigh, daughter of Estelle. You have invoked the Raphilian Rite to have this audience. What is it you seek?"

His tone is so... neutral. I can't hear any judgment. No approval or disapproval. Nothing. It gives me no indication of how to proceed. I stand taller and draw in a fortifying breath.

"Thank you. I understand that humans are typically terminated in cases where they have been exposed to the more difficult-to-wipe situations relating to our world. I would request that Henry be spared from this fate. To be left alone. I trust him. He won't expose us."

The room is silent beyond comfort. After what feels like an eternity, Solomon, the Arch Mage, shatters it.

"I do not think it provides any advantage to our world to bend the rules in this instance. I, for one, am surprised by your choice to include the human in the first place considering your past, Miss Cole."

I shift uneasily, wanting to refute Solomon, but something in my gut tells me I should wait. Experience has taught me to listen to my intuition. It's not quite the same as when I get visions, but I listen all the same.

Iridessa shakes her head, all soft lines and regret. "I see no benefit to the supernatural world from allowing this to happen."

I suck my lips in between my teeth, fighting the urge to bite back at the callous way they are discussing my friend's life, human or not.

"Considering Miss Cole's past, I doubt she'd vouch for someone who'd expose us. We've granted exceptions before," the Werewolf King offers.

I nod gratefully to him, and I see Alaric give an almost imperceptible nod as well. Interesting. Maybe some things have changed for him since we last met in Paris.

"I am inclined to agree with Conall," Raphael adds, his tone still neutral.

Orpheus taps a nail on his table, pulling the attention of the room, though this time he avoids looking at me. "I believe we are too compromised already to risk another breach in the same locality."

My heart races. With only the Ruler of Demons and the High Witch left to speak, this could go horribly wrong. I remind myself to keep focusing and check in on Henry. He's looking at me, terror shining from his eyes—terror for me instead of the terror he should have for himself, and my fingers grow clammy.

Nicon looks at Henry and then back to me, his face lined with amusement and a twinkle of mischief lights his eyes. "I think the fun is yet to come. I say let him live and we'll see what happens."

Octavia lets out a small huff as she surveys me and Henry. I wait impatiently, despite my senses telling me this will go in our favor. I love it when my angelic gifts decide to weigh in at an opportune time.

"It seems this decision falls to me then. I think considering the losses Miss Cole has already experienced, leniency is in order." Octavia nods to me and then looks directly at Henry. "There is a trial currently running that I think the human will be suitable to join."

The other Council members simultaneously stiffen and their heads whip to Octavia. Clearly, her decision is unexpected.

Octavia ignores the others and continues as though they didn't just give such a big reaction. "We are currently determining the human reaction to our existence in small samples. I would like you to attend the front desk on the eighteenth floor and they will present you with an information package on the program. I will check on your progress personally. Understood?"

Henry seems lost for words but manages to nod in response. My muscles relax a little, but I remain curious about why Octavia would mention this in front of me and Alaric. Perhaps that's why the Council members reacted the way they did in response to her mentioning it.

She looks back at me. "Miss Cole, I request that you leave Henry to attend this appointment on his own. Also, neither you nor Alaric should mention the existence of the trial outside of this room. Is that clear?"

"Yes. I understand."

Alaric offers a mid-level bow and simply says, "Yes, ma'am."

After a moment of silence, Raphael stands. "Alaric, I believe you are free to go. Drop Henry to the eighteenth floor on your way out. Miss Cole, I will speak with you in my office on the floor below us in a moment. Please go there now."

I let out a mute sigh of relief, glad to get the hells out of this room. A small smile pulls my lips up as I daydream of returning to my quiet life with the humans, but it passes quickly.

I'm just not that lucky.

Raphael stands looking out of his office window when I enter. He turns and meets my eyes, his face more curious than neutral now that he's away from the rest of the Council members. "Miss Cole, please take a seat." He gestures at the light gray lounge chair on my right, and I move towards it.

Trying to fake a calmness I don't feel about agreeing to be locked to Raphael for the next one hundred years, I attempt to give myself a few moments. "I'd prefer Everleigh, please. If that is all right?"

He nods briefly as he takes a seat. His white-blond hair captures the light of the sun and manages to look metallic. He looks so perfect it's unnatural, but the hint of emotion on his face makes him look all too real.

"I assume you are wondering about what happened with both Orpheus and myself in the meeting upstairs." At my nod, he continues. "I am unsure why Orpheus chose to do so, particularly in a Council meeting, however it seems he attempted to enthrall you in some way—to influence you. Though it appears all he did was make you faint. I will make discreet inquiries. I am sure you understand asking such things directly would not be wise. Did you hear anything in your mind at the time?"

I slowly shake my head. "No, nothing. Why would he try such a thing so openly?"

"I am not sure. Though, I think we could draw the conclusion that your response was unexpected."

Not wanting to push any harder about this matter, since he's already offered to look into it, which is more than he needs to do, I focus on his other point. "And what happened... with our eyes?"

He tilts his head slightly to the left and looks directly into my eyes. I feel my glow pull through, and a gold hue from my eyes reflects in the small coffee table before me. Then, as if they can't help it, Raphael's eyes light up as well.

"It's curious. Typically, such a pull can only be forced by someone of my bloodline, but I knew Estelle, your mother." His voice lowers. "This response never happened with her. I do not know why it has happened with you. Do you know if you were gifted with any power from someone of my line?"

I pull my lips between my teeth and try to remember anything my mother or father may have mentioned but come up blank. "No, I don't believe so. Nothing I can recall anyway." I wonder if the same thing would happen with Clara.

"I have met your sister, Clara, at her place of work, and this did not happen with her," he offers.

Can he read my mind or something?

A single chuckle breaks free of Raphael, and I can't help but lean towards him. "It seems as if we were having similar thoughts. I don't read minds if that is what you wondered next."

I relax into the seat, glad my thoughts are still my own, even if it seems to amuse him more. He looks so much more... human away from the Council. When his features harden, I sit up straighter again, my heart racing as I realize it's time for the real reason I am in his office.

"You are aware of the cost for enacting the Rite."

I nod, heart thudding against my chest so hard I'm sure he can hear it. "Fealty for one hundred years or until you consider the Rite fulfilled."

He returns a small bow of his head and answers in an interested tone, "I know from lack of hearing about you that you have avoided being involved with the supernatural world. Is this human's life truly worth it?"

"Yes," I answer immediately. "It will always be worth it to spare a life." After a moment, I add quietly, "Though I have managed to do that without breaking the rules until now. But he is a good friend."

Raphael's face remains neutral as he says, "Befriending humans for our ten-year stays before moving is not recommended."

"I know. But the human role I am currently employed to do—that of a psychologist—I can't do alone."

He stares at me for long enough that I begin to feel edgy, waiting for him to tell me what I will be required to do during my fealty period.

"For now, I would like you to return to your role at the psychology clinic. But when you are not working, I would like you to look into the missing humans. I believe there is more going on here than meets the eye, and it is not something I can look into myself. You should report back to me directly with anything you find. Do not tell anyone about what I have asked of you. No matter what. I will find you when it is time. After that... we will see."

I breathe an internal sigh of relief that he hasn't decided to make me pack up and leave my life immediately, but I make sure to keep the reaction from my face the best I can. Raphael is known to be fair, but I've never found giving away too much around another supe smart. Especially not the earthly leader of an entire species.

BROKEN

I SENSE THE MAGIC the moment I enter my office. It's subtle but I'm immediately on alert. I scan the room from my place at the door, starting at the floor in front of me and expanding across the space until I spot a very dim glow emanating from the top of my desk. I approach cautiously, and when I'm near enough to see what it is, I huff out a breath.

It's just a letter. The sliver of magic attached to the parchment—so outdated—means only supes can see it. It has my name scrawled on the front, and I flip it over. The wax seal has the insignia of the Accord Enforcement Office—handcuffs, just a subtle reminder. I shake my head at this archaic practice despite the Council regularly using technology and magic to achieve their goals.

I crack the seal and my view of the room disappears until all I can see is white. *Great. A vision.* I rest a hand on the table and wait for it to take form.

It's pitch black wherever I am, and the sound of a bone being snapped causes a shiver to cascade through my body. Then nothing. I blink. A faint light comes from a crescent moon, and I look around. All I see are graves for miles. No people. Just graves.

I'm back in the room. Fear crashes into me—the sensation threatening to overwhelm my senses. I lean on my desk to breathe through the onslaught of emotions. Once my racing heart returns to normal, I consider the vision. Clearly, someone has been killed and buried, but there's nothing else I can recall that might tell me who it was or why it happened. Frustration burns in my chest knowing I don't have enough information to help whoever it is, and I curse my erratic powers again.

Why can't they just work reliably? How am I supposed to help anyone like this?

I close my eyes again and search for any details that might tell me where the vision took place, but I draw a blank. A heaviness in my chest weighs me down. I still have a client missing and likely more murder victims to find. A part of me hopes that more of the vision will show itself but, given the propensity of my visions showing up too late to intervene, another part of me hopes it never comes back.

I turn my attention back to the parchment in front of me and finish opening it. Sure enough, it's a letter from Alaric, albeit a short one.

All deceased clients have been listed as missing persons in the police database by our tech team and assigned to one of our officers. Don't log anything further at your workplace or talk to anyone about them. Henry knows too. Reach out if you hear anything about your

***other missing client or if more fail to attend their
appointments. Alaric.***

I frown at the paper. Annoyance and sadness well up at the
way people are treated by the supernatural community. Supes
mostly have long existences, but the disregard for humans has
always been a weight on my heart. Just because they aren't here
for as long as we are doesn't mean they're worth any less. The
love humans have for their lives is another reason I enjoy their
company. They seem to care more.

Well, most of them.

A shiver runs down my spine as I think of some of the more
heinous humans I've come across in my past. Determined not
to dwell on it, I shift my focus back to my workplace and get
ready for my day of clients.

I clock out at the end of the day exhausted. All my clients
showed up despite my growing concern they wouldn't. There
was also no news about Sophie.

Feeling down, I stop in at Henry's office to check on him, but
as I approach, I see the lights in his office are out. He's either
gone for the day or he never came in. My brows draw down and
I try to smooth them out before walking through the reception

foyer, intending to call or stop in and see him at home. I wave at the last of the front desk staff still working, and head down in the elevator.

On the street, I pull out my phone, search for Henry's number, and hit Call. After a moment, it starts ringing. Two cycles later, it cuts to message bank and my stomach tightens in fear. Maybe the Council didn't tell the truth. Maybe he isn't okay. But before I can wind myself up into a complete panic, my phone vibrates with a message.

Henry: Sorry, Ev. Can't talk. Working through the package with... the ones from that place? Talk soon. I'm okay. – H

I roll my shoulders back, determined to get home so I can stretch out my wings and find some relief. The internal knots I'm developing from all this stress are killing me.

First, I have a stop to make.

I jump into a cab—one of my least favorite activities when they drive like maniacs—and ask to be dropped at an address close to the Accord building.

Once I make it inside, I head straight to the desk.

"I'd like to speak with Alaric Bane, please."

The fae male, who looks good enough to eat poisonous fruit off, eyes me with a lustful gaze, and I'm immediately taken aback and suspicious of his interest.

Put him down just in case. It's not worth the risk.

"Of course," he murmurs, voice husky. "I'll see if he's available. Please take a seat." He gestures to the lounge chairs.

I pinch the skin of my opposite hand trying to focus on the present instead of my inner demon side so that we can both keep our head. I walk over and wait, careful to keep half an eye on the fae.

After what feels like twenty years, Alaric steps out of the lift and walks over to me. "I didn't expect to see you so soon. Has something happened?"

I try not to let his grumbling, accusatory tone bother me because I'm sure it has more to do with the case than with me. The last time he "helped" me deal with a case, he was fanatical about following leads and capturing the treacherous fae who were causing the problems. It seems no less likely he will be running down the leads on this case with just as much ferocity.

"No," I reply. "There's nothing new, but I wanted to know what my clients' families will be told at the end of this case."

Alaric's features smooth to political neutrality. "The victims will remain listed as missing. You know that."

Like hells, wolf!

I shake my head. "No, Alaric. Not this time. I had to watch the families in Paris worry for years over whether their loved ones would ever return. I'm not doing it again. They deserve to at least know they're gone. In an accident or something. Something that won't tarnish their memories."

He stares at me, looking ready to say something, but seems to stop himself. After a moment, he answers. "You know the rules, Miss Cole. We don't do that."

"Don't give me that shit, Alaric, exceptions can be made. I won't let this happen. Either you tell the families something, or I will." Despite my best efforts, I feel heat build in my eyes, and I know from experience they've turned the same red as my father's eyes. The same red Clara uses to intimidate patrons at the bar she works in.

When he looks like he's going to argue with me, angry heat rises to my cheeks and I cut him off before he can speak. "Seriously, Alaric. This is my only warning. Sort something out—or I will."

I turn on my heel and walk out, focusing my energy on trying to get my eyes to return to their normal shade before I reach the ward back to the human street.

I really haven't missed this supernatural shit.

Who needs sleep?

I wake exhausted from my once-a-week night of sleep, feeling worse than I did before I went to bed. I rub the sleep—or lack thereof—from my eyes and try to piece together my overnight memories. Basically, what was vision and what were simply nightmares. I prefer when my visions come during the day, because then I don't have to worry about sorting fact from fiction when I wake up. But, as always, my powers seem to have a mind of their own. Or maybe a motivation of their own? I close my eyes again and try to remember.

Pitch black. A bone snapping. The graveyard.
Blood. Torn, crimson throats. Moonlight. A park.
Fangs dripping blood. Auburn hair. Short. Curly.
Sophie!

No! I jump from the bed and rip the curtain back. It's still nighttime. I need to get to the park. Maybe I can stop her.

I pull my running shoes on, cursing the law to stay hidden, because running to this park instead of flying is going to cost me precious time.

I fling the front door shut behind me and haul ass down the stairs, grateful for once that I'm only on the third floor. Once out of the apartment building, I head south. Casting my mind back to the vision, I try to pin down the exact section of the park I need to search. The view of the water and the position of the trees in the vision are enough to give me a pretty good idea.

I approach the park at a run, determined to stop whatever this is if I can. My stomach sinks as I smell the harsh tang of iron in the air. I round the miniature forest of trees and am met with the blood-tinged amber eyes of Sophie. My heart and lungs are so constricted it's hard to breathe. I throw my hands up to show her I'm not here to hurt her.

"Sophie. It's me. Everleigh. Can you let me help you?"

She viciously shakes her head as bloodied tears stream down her face.

"I'm a monster," she whispers. "I can't stop."

She sucks in a ragged breath as she looks at the two bodies beneath her. They have their throats torn out, just like in my vision. A little blood pools around their bodies, but it seems like Sophie has consumed most of it.

"It's okay, Sophie. It's not your fault. Let me help—"

Sophie screeches and jerks backward, suddenly in pain. She grabs her arm, and I whirl around to figure out what happened.

Fucking wolfman!

"Alaric," I hiss. "What in the hells are you doing?"

His icy eyes lock with mine as he reloads his crossbow with another wooden bolt.

I move from my position and stand in his way while Sophie recovers. I can still save her.

"Get out of the way, Everleigh. I'm doing my job. This body count has to stop, and you know it."

There's a rustle behind me but I can't look. My gaze is trained on Alaric and his murder weapon, and my breathing is so shallow I'm beginning to feel faint. "We can help her, Alaric. It doesn't need to end like this."

He lets out an exasperated sigh and lowers his weapon. I use the time to look behind me. Sophie's gone. I bow my head and squeeze my eyes tight for a moment, working to return my breathing to normal.

"What in the hellish realms are you doing here, Everleigh? You're impeding an active investigation. I don't care if she was your client. If you don't stay out of the way, I'll have no choice but to have you detained until I can put this case to bed."

I pinch my lips together and try to maintain a façade of calm. "I had a vision. I tried to get here in time to stop it from happening. Was I supposed to waste precious time sitting on hold with the Council office to notify you?"

He storms towards me, pulls a card from his pocket, and shoves it toward me. "Call me directly or send a message. Your client can't keep killing innocent people. She needs to be stopped, and I need to find her maker so they can be stopped as well. You—"

A shrill ring cuts Alaric off and he pulls his phone from his jeans. How he fits in anything extra with all the muscles he already has packed in is beyond me.

He turns from me as he answers. "Yes?"

I look at the bodies of what appear to be a couple in their early twenties and hang my head, holding back tears.

Trying to help always seems to come at a cost.

"You're fucking kidding me. Right. Send me the photos."

I raise my brows in question, and, to my surprise, he actually answers the look I give him. This case must really be getting to him.

"There's another baby vamp on the loose. More bodies were picked up across town at the same time we arrived here. Fresh. Sophie can't have been in two places at once. It looks like there's a master vamp who also needs to be put down."

I tilt my head slightly. "How can you be sure it's the same one?"

He folds his arms defensively. "There's no guarantee but, in my experience, the likelihood of two separate masters illegally turning people in the same city around the same time are about slim to none."

Despite my better judgment, I offer, "Do you need any help?"

Alaric's piercing, icy gaze flings back to me. "No," he says in a tone as sharp as a knife. "This isn't your job. We have a team for this, and you need to stay out of the way. And don't be showing up to potential crime scenes—visions or not. Send a message or call. We will follow it up. Understood?"

Holy hells you're infuriating.

I stare at him for a moment and fight the rising red glow itching to break free from my eyes. I ground out a professional but noncommittal response. "I understand what you're saying."

He looks like he's going to say more, but for the second time today, I don't have the patience for it. I turn and leave, heading back the way I came.

If he thinks I'm not going to try and save Sophie, he's got another thing coming.

Sitting on the couch in my apartment, my mind is pulled back to my time in Paris fifty years ago, and my body feels heavy with guilt and sadness. Jean, Beau, Elodie, Gabriel, Fleur, and Louis—all dead because they were my clients. And it nearly killed me watching them slowly go insane after Kairain—one of the fae who knew and hated my father—poisoned them with fae foods just to get at me. I was too slow to figure out what was going on and my visions were so irregular and nonspecific that I didn't have enough information until it was too late.

I replay the day Alaric came to my door in Paris fifty years ago. After a few weeks of working together to discover what was going on with my clients, he'd arrived looking stoic as all hells. He told me those clients and Kairain had been put down. Their insanity had rendered them too dangerous to live. None of the elder fae or witches on retainer for the Council could save them.

"What about their families?" I'd asked him. "What will they be told?"

The emptiness in his eyes jarred me into speechlessness. I remember wondering how he could be so cold when he said they'd be told nothing. Like they didn't matter. The victims would just be known as missing persons. It was *easier* to list people with mental health and addiction problems as missing. Protocol. The injustice still grates on me. I watched over their families for years from a distance. A few of them succumbed to suicide when they couldn't find their loved ones. Never have I hated the laws as much as I did on those days.

Those losses remind me that staying away from the supernatural community is best. Some of the fae are just savages. So many supes don't care about human lives. It burns me on the inside.

I shake my head to pull myself out of the past. Being made aware that a newly turned vampire is responsible, one I don't know, eases some of my guilt.

Maybe this isn't my fault. My family's fault. I can't be the reason more lives are lost.

I know it's selfish to feel relief but losing the people I know, especially the ones in my care, is a heavy burden to carry. I need to exercise to get out of my head while I wait and, for the first time, hope for a vision to help me find Sophie before Alaric does.

It's Saturday morning and I still haven't found another trace of Sophie either through a vision or by calling people she knows. The uneasy, slightly sick feeling in my stomach still bothers me too. The vision of how she'd looked, with blood dripping down her face and fear in her eyes, won't leave my mind.

The antique grandmother clock on my living room wall chimes to tell me it's nine o'clock. At the same time, my doorbell buzzes loudly, and I jump up, unsure who would be visiting. I pull the door open, and my heart lightens immediately.

"Henry! Come in!" I step back so he can enter and as soon as I shut the door behind him, I give him a tight hug. "I've been so worried. Are you okay?"

I take him in, dressed in his usual pants and suspenders despite it being the weekend. He has dark smudges under his eyes but otherwise appears to be much the same.

"It's good to see you, Ev. I'm sorry I haven't spoken to you since that text. I had to go through a bunch of the stuff they gave me after that... meeting. And then I just... I needed time to process, you know?"

I nod quickly. "Are you coping with it all okay? I mean, I understand it's a lot to take in. I'm here for you still, if you want me to be?"

He reaches out and takes one of my hands, and despite everything he's been through, his genuineness and compassion shine through.

"I'm getting there. I don't blame you. You know my view of life. It is what it is. It's not about blame. Please don't be hard on yourself."

Heat rises into my eyes and I marvel at the potential goodness in humanity. At their ability to be like Henry should they choose to, despite—or maybe because of—their short lives.

"Thank you, Henry. And really, if there is anything you need, I'm here for you."

He's quiet for a moment, and I can see a question forming behind his eyes. I wait but I have a decent idea what might be coming next.

Henry stares into my eyes with his warm brown ones. The lines around them and his pale-yellow aura tell me he's curious, and the tiniest tinge of orange says perhaps a little guarded or nervous.

"You didn't get to tell me before, and I got a bit of an idea from the Council, but would you—and you don't have to—but would you tell me what you are?"

I smile gently even as apprehension flares to life about the possible impact of telling him, but then remind myself he's already my friend and this shouldn't change anything. I gesture over at my couches and grab a couple of sodas from the fridge. I pass his over and sit opposite him, the table between us feeling like one of the barriers we try to avoid in therapy sessions.

"I don't think there's an easier way of doing this, so I'll just come out and say it. I'm half angel and half demon."

He looks back at me, his face carefully blank and calm as if we're in a therapy session. I feel one side of my mouth creep up, amusement distracting me for a fraction of a second. He smiles in return, seemingly unable to stop himself, and my expression builds to match his. The moment passes when his brows scrunch together, clearly thinking something through.

"Wait. In all of these lesson thingies I've had to do, they never talked about half anythings. Is that, like, normal?"

My shoulders drop a little as I deflate back into the lounge and curl my legs up. It seems he knows enough.

"No. It's not normal. Hybrids are against our laws because the recorded histories of such things have been... problematic."

"What do you mean?"

I draw in a breath until my lungs inflate fully before huffing it back out.

"Well, when species mix—and not all of them can do it—there are usually magical problems. Like, for me..." I swallow the lump in my throat. "I get visions, like most angels, but they don't work like they should. Usually visions come as whole 'scenes,' that have all the information you might need about a person or an issue. But mine just kind of... come in unhelpful snippets that often miss important details, like the *who* or the *where*."

Henry scrunches his nose. "I'm sorry, Ev. That must be tough. Seems like fitting in would have been hard enough for you without that problem too."

"Thanks, Henry. Yeah, it's not been the easiest. I don't really fit in with the angels or demons, even if I look a little more angelic than my sister."

He frowns for a moment, then his eyes widen. "Oh, of course. So, Clara is half and half too." He laughs and looks at me meaningfully then winks. "More demon, though, I guess."

I laugh despite myself. "Yes, but she wouldn't thank you for saying so."

He sits forward in his chair and a sheen of excitement lights his features. "Does this mean you have wings?"

A smile builds again on my face. Henry really has a way of keeping things light and happy, even when circumstances aren't so great. "I do. Would you like to see them?"

"You bet!"

I laugh and stand, then head to the windows and close the blackout blinds. I paid extra to have electronic shutters put onto the outside so I could have more privacy when I moved to town, and I put those down too. When I'm sure everything is secure, I go back to the living room and turn my back to Henry, then look over my shoulder at him.

"You ready?"

"Absolutely," he says, his tone high with excitement.

With very little effort, I access the ether and release my wings, grateful for the way my clothing morphs to accommodate them. I stretch them out as far as the room allows, relishing the freedom of the moment. The tension in the muscles between them relaxes. There's just something about having my wings out that makes me feel comfortable and at ease.

Henry stands and wonder shines from him, his aura a similar shade as the pearlescent white of my wings.

"They're so... beautiful? That word doesn't seem like enough. Magical? Magnificent?"

I chuckle quietly as happiness and contentment swell inside me. It's been so long since anyone has seen my wings and not hated them, unable to see past my DNA. My lips tilt down as I remember the way angels and demons alike would sneer because I was never pure enough or good enough for either of them. Always less than and never fitting in.

Annoyed at myself, I draw my wings together to pull them back into the ether, and Henry gasps. The sound ricochets around in my head as my view shades to white and a new vision fills my mind.

FATE

I STAND IN THE same graveyard again. Dim light comes from the crescent moon, and I take a moment to look around. I'm in the older part of the cemetery; there are a few crumbling mausoleums and large statues that new graveyards don't have the space for anymore. Or maybe people don't have the money for them. I close my eyes and listen. A faint sound of moving water—perhaps boats upsetting the flow of the harbor—is in the background, but a closer noise stops my heart. I look down and see the dirt of a freshly disturbed grave begin to ripple.

"Shit!"

My sight returns and Henry is right in front of me, waving his hand in front of my eyes.

"Are you okay, Ev? You kind of just zoned out or something."

"Vision," I mutter as I step around Henry. "I'm okay. I just need my phone. Sorry."

I grab it off the kitchen counter and stare at it for a moment while doubt pools in my stomach. Telling Alaric about my latest vision might not be the smartest choice, but maybe it will get me some leverage to help Sophie. I search for his number and hit the Call button.

"Just give me a minute," I say to Henry, and walk to my bedroom when he nods.

Alaric answers without preamble. "Do you know something new?"

I ignore his unpleasantness for the sake of the situation. "I've had another vision. I think someone else is going to be turned." I glance at the calendar on my wall to check the moon cycle. "Sometime in the next night or two."

He mutters some expletives before addressing me again, his tone careful since he knows about my vision issues from Paris. "Do you have anything we can use to find them?"

I sigh. "Not a lot. All I can get is that they'll be buried in the older part of a cemetery, close enough to the water I could hear it but far enough away you couldn't see it if you were at the grave. The dirt had been freshly disturbed. You know the master only needs to bury their progeny overnight, so based on the vision, they'll be turned and buried tonight or tomorrow night at the latest."

He's quiet for a few moments longer. "I think there are only a couple of graveyards that fit the bill. I'll organize a search. Call if you get anything else." He pauses again like he's going to say something, but then he ends the call.

"Asshole," I mutter.

I go back out to find Henry on the couch sipping his drink and waiting for me.

"Sorry, Henry. I just had a vision and I needed to relay the information to Alaric."

He nods. "Will it help with the case, do you think?"

"I'm not sure. It might help narrow things down to find someone, but I don't know if it will be of any use in the bigger picture or not."

Frustrated, I throw myself down on the couch opposite Henry and have some of my drink. He leaves me to my thoughts for a minute before I notice his leg bouncing up and down. I look at him expectantly.

"Have you heard anything at all?" he asks. "About Sophie, I mean."

I freeze, unsure what to say. Knowing about our world doesn't mean he should know everything. Especially all the bad stuff. Not when it's all still so new to him.

"I can see that's a tough question to answer," he says. "Sorry, Ev. It's okay. I'm sure you'll tell me what you can when you can."

Indecision wars within me but, eventually, I nod. "I will. When the time is right. Sorry, Henry. I know a lot is going on for you right now."

He grimaces and checks his watch. "Speaking of. I need to get going actually. I have a meeting with that older witch lady. You know, the one from the meeting. Octavia something?"

My brows draw up. "You have a meeting with Octavia Witt?"

"Yeah. Remember she said she'd check my progress or whatever herself? So, I'm meeting her for that. She's coming to me, though." He stops and frowns for a moment before adding, "Should I do anything before she comes? To be polite or safe or whatever? Or not offend her at least? Do witches, like, drink anything special?"

I practice my therapy poker face to avoid showing any amusement, so he doesn't feel judged for asking. "Well, I'd say in terms of being safe, not really, but I don't imagine you have anything to worry about from her. She's the one who invited you to the program. Just be honest and confident, if you can. Use your psychologist's face—don't give too much away. That's always the smartest option in the supernatural world. And, uh, as for a drink, we're just as varied as the humans. I doubt she'll take anything, though. Trust also isn't a strong suit."

He nods, seemingly grateful for the advice but perhaps too overwhelmed to talk about it. "Okay. I'm gonna head off. Provided all goes well today, I'll be back to work on Monday, all right? Maybe we can get that pasta we never got around to."

"It sounds like a good idea." I smile as I walk him to the door. "You be safe and call if you need me, okay?"

He gives me a quick hug. "Of course. See ya, Ev." Then he makes his way out the door.

I try all afternoon to get the vision to come back in the hopes I can see a name on the gravestone or something useful. But nothing I replay from my conversation with Henry makes it happen. When scrolling through graveyard and funeral websites doesn't prove fruitful either, I decide to text Alaric.

Me: Have you had any luck with finding the grave?
Alaric: No.
Me: Will you tell me if you do?
Alaric: No. Stay out of it.

Should just bite him into submission.

That's hardly going to help.

He's a walking conundrum these days. In Paris he was cold, stoic, and didn't give an inch. Now, he seems to have emotions and he's shown a little care, and even though he argues with me, he still seems to have listened. He's also obstinate, emotionless, and refuses to share information. Surely working together would be more useful.

When it's time to eat a late dinner, I order pizza because I'm too agitated to cook. As soon as I pick up my phone, a vision starts, and I stop trying to open the app as I wait, equal parts fear and anticipation.

Sophie stares up at me over two bodies in the same park as yesterday. Teenagers. She's crying blood. Looking at her hands. Suddenly, she looks up at me. "Help me. Please."

Wings flutter up a storm inside my stomach. It wasn't the vision I thought was coming, but it's the one I need. Shoes already on from my walk earlier, I rush out the door. I don't bother to text Alaric this time. I'm determined to save her.

I rush to the park and panic a little when I see my vision is already taking place. It's surreal when my visions align exactly with reality. I approach slowly and lower myself to my knees on the ground a few paces away.

"Sophie," I whisper. "Sophie? I'm here. Talk to me."

Her bloody face and eyes filled with terror are knives to my heart, and I wish I could undo everything she's been through.

"E-E-Everleigh. What's happened to me? What's wrong with me? Why am I doing this? Why can't I stop?" Her voice gets more shrill with each word as panic commandeers her system, pulling her further from rational thought.

"Shh, Sophie. It will be okay. I can explain it to you. I promise it will be okay. Why don't you come with me? We can get you cleaned up. Talk."

I keep my words calm, gentle, and soothing. Loud enough that she can hear me over the water but soft enough not to frighten her.

Her gaze flicks up behind me, and a snarl rips from her mouth as I spin around to see what she noticed. As I turn, the air ripples and I watch in horror as a sharp wooden bolt flies past my face. I hear a solid thud followed by the tearing of skin as it plunges into her. He doesn't miss this time. It's a heart shot. I don't spare him a glance as I run toward Sophie. She hits the ground, immediately turning white in true death, and a fracture runs through my heart.

Pain. Sorrow. Anger.

I get up from the ground and turn to face Alaric, the heat in my eyes letting me know they're blazing red. I run straight at him. In range, I curl my hands into fists, thumb wrapped tightly to the outside, and throw my first punch. It makes a satisfying crunch when it connects with his nose. He doesn't allow another, but it doesn't stop me. I throw punch after punch.

"What." *Hit.* "The." *Hit.* "Hells." *Hit.* "Is." *Hit.* "Wrong." *Hit.* "With." *Hit.* "You?"

I can't stop myself. I'm so angry. So crushed.

Alaric doesn't fight back. Just blocks his face from another blow. He takes the hits and grunts as he absorbs the supernatural strength of each punch.

Eventually, I stop, and I realize I'm crying. The red glow from my eyes is gone and there's blood on my knuckles. I look at them, then at him. There's blood on him. When I speak next, my voice sounds as broken as I feel on the inside.

"How could you do this? I could have helped her."

I see him flinch, just the slightest movement around his eyes, but his voice is monotone. "I didn't have a choice. The order was given by the Vampire King. She'd killed too many already and she had to be put down."

I keep my eyes open wide, trying to stop the flow of tears. "*Put down*? Like she's some kind of animal? She wasn't an animal, Alaric." I suck in a sob. "She was a person with a family. She didn't deserve this. Didn't you see how terrified she was? Did you even care?"

He seems to hollow out in front of me and part of me feels good about it. Like he deserves it. Another part of me sees the hurt my question has caused.

Dammit. Couldn't he just stay emotionless?

Unable to stand here anymore, I take one last look at Sophie while more tears run freely, burning a path down my cheeks, and then turn to make my way home.

"Everleigh?" Alaric calls softly.

I stop, unable to ignore the rare note of emotion in his voice, but I don't say anything.

"For what it's worth, I am sorry. I know this isn't what you wanted."

After freezing a moment longer, considering his pain and his words, I nod, still not turning around. I don't have anything else to say right now.

The next night, I'm still in the same clothes and drowning in the sorrow of not being able to help a single one of my missing clients, who are now all dead. But then I flick on the evening news, and I get a better understanding of why Alaric was given his orders. More than fifteen people have gone missing recently in the local area around Darling Harbour. Numbers that high are causing panic in the human world. Which means the supernatural community is being monitored more closely, the rules and punishments are stricter, and I'm willing to bet that more supes than just Alaric will be on this case now.

I hate what he did, even if it was his job.

I switch off the television and fling the remote to the other end of the couch. There is at least one other baby blood sucker on the loose that Alaric got the phone call about, and another that I know will rise incredibly soon.

I turn my mind back to the other vision I had—the one of the newly turned vampire—and wonder if the master vamp has turned them because Alaric killed Sophie or if they're just building their numbers. It wouldn't be the first time one of them tried to build their own little army to get what they wanted. Not that it had ever turned out well. I shake my head, trying to physically make my chaotic mind focus.

Either tonight or tomorrow night, that vampire will rise. *Maybe I can help them, even if I couldn't help Sophie or my other clients.*

With a little purpose leaking in, I jump up and take a quick shower, then pull on some dark clothes and set off. My destination is the graveyard I found online that resembles the one from my vision, though it's in another part of the city to

Darling Harbour. There were closer ones without water views, but my gut feeling says I should go to this one, so I get a cab.

It's dark by the time I arrive, and I'm grateful I bought a flashlight with me. My wings might be a better light source since they glow, but the Council would hardly accept that as a valid reason to pull them out here. The last lot of angelic sightings caused quite a surge in the book industry despite the supernatural enforcement officers working overtime to shut that down. Thankfully, the media sensationalized it and the stories were spun as digital enhancements.

It wasn't a pretty punishment for the angel either.

I wander through the rows of graves, looking for something familiar. Anything. But these graves are too new to be the ones in my vision. My instinct tells me I'm in the right place, so I keep trekking through. At forty-one acres, it's not a small area to cover on foot, especially by myself in the dark with a flashlight.

I suppose letting Alaric know about my hunch could be helpful to focus the enforcement officer's efforts, but I don't want to see him again so soon, nor do I want the new vamp to be put down without an offer of help.

Okay then. On my own it is.

After another hour of searching, the moon appears from behind thick clouds, just as it did in my vision. My heart races, wanting to find the vamp before they leave the graveyard. Their new master should be here to help them, but I'm getting the impression they won't be, partly because I didn't see them in my vision, and partly because they have let the other two, that I know about, run free.

Finally, I reach the area of the graveyard that looks familiar, and I walk along the rows, doing my best to look and listen for the subtlest of noises. After several minutes, a quiet gasping sob breaks the silence, and I rush towards it, certain that the only being I'll find here tonight is the newly turned vampire.

On the outskirts of the flashlight beam, I see a filthy, dirt-caked young woman with reddish-brown hair. Her clothes are torn in places and smeared with blood despite her skin being completely unbroken. She sits jammed back into the tombstone behind her, knees pulled up to her chest, one arm around her legs and the other clasping her throat. Her eyes are pools of sheer panic when they meet mine.

"What—" She tries to cough to clear the rasp from her voice. "What's wrong with me? Why am I here? Why does it hurt so much?"

I squat down a few paces away, taking care not to get too close and risk being attacked. The last thing she needs is to be made to feel worse about what's happening to her right now.

"What do you remember?"

The panic fades from her eyes and instead, she looks lost, vulnerable, and young.

"I... was out on a date, I think. I don't normally do that." She pauses and stares at me until I nod in understanding. "Then when I left to go back to my car, someone attacked me." Her voice shakes and blood-stained tears roll down her cheeks. She reaches up and wipes them. The moment she realizes the tears aren't normal, her panic returns.

"It's going to be okay," I say gently, trying to be reassuring with my words and my tone. "I can explain what's going on. I can help you, if you let me. I know this is terrifying, but it will be okay."

She sucks in a sharp breath and nods back at me as she continues clutching her throat. "Who are you?"

"I'm Everleigh. Everleigh Cole. I'm a psychologist. Could you tell me your name?"

She pauses for a second, seemingly searching through her erratic thoughts for the answer to my question. "I'm Raine Pillari. I'm a schoolteacher in the city."

"Hi, Raine. Thanks for telling me your name. Would you like to get out of the cemetery? Then I can explain what's going on and help with your sore throat?"

She startles, and her tone becomes suspicious and increasingly panicked with each word. "Wait. What are you doing here? How do you know what's wrong with my throat? Did you do this to me?"

"No. I didn't. I promise, Raine," I say calmly. "I'm just someone who can help you. Maybe a... guardian angel of sorts, if you like?"

Her movements appear to be slowing, and a pit begins to hollow out in my stomach. She needs blood. And soon.

"Please. I promise I can help. Let's just get out of the cemetery before anyone comes looking through here, okay?"

After a moment's hesitation, she nods and begins to stand. I move around the empty grave and offer her a hand, which she takes. After pulling her up toward me, I see her nose scrunch up—clearly, I don't smell so good to her. Humans will, though. We need to avoid people. This is going to be tough.

I lead Raine back down the row of graves and toward a small road. Once we walk out from behind the last mausoleum, I stop and pull her to a halt with me.

Alaric.

I glare at him. "What in the deepest layer of the hells are you doing here? How did you know where I was?"

He folds his arms over his chest, causing his biceps to bulge and catch my eye. "It's none of your concern. Hand her over."

My brows recede into my hairline as Raine gasps and pulls on me, trying to back away. I grasp her hand in mine and wait until she makes eye contact with me.

"I've got you, okay? I won't hand you over or do anything else you don't feel safe doing."

I ignore the snort from Alaric and wait until Raine acknowledges my words and relaxes again. Then I turn back to Alaric.

"You're dreaming. I'm not letting her out of my sight right now. She needs help. Not what you have planned for her."

I hear his foot grind into the gravel and catch the shock on Raine's face when she realizes she heard such a subtle movement too. I grasp her hand more tightly, offering support the best way

I can while trying to deal with the hulking wolf-man in front of us.

"You need to stay out of this, Everleigh. Steps need to be taken. I have a responsibility here. This is my job. Not yours."

Over my dead body.

I bend my left knee, and my right hip juts out. "You're not taking her, Alaric."

He steps forward, and Raine begins to quiver. "Yes. I am."

I shift her behind me in a clear show of defiance, bending my knees to rest in a defensive stance.

"Over my dead body, Alaric. You'll have to kill me first. I refuse to let her pay for the crimes of a rogue vampire."

His gaze locks with mine, and I feel a jolt run through me at his heated gaze. His voice, originally emotionless, now seems to hold a flicker of the warmth in his eyes.

"And what exactly do you propose, Everleigh?"

The way he says my name makes desire pulse in my core, and I lose a touch of my bravado. "She comes with me. I'll explain things. Once she's settled, we can come in together. Then you can ask her your questions."

One side of his lips curves up for a split second, leaving me wondering if I was just imagining it. "No good. Orpheus is not so lenient that you can just waltz off and show up whenever you like. This needs to be sorted out." His tone shifts again, seriousness taking over. "There are too many missing already."

I sigh, reluctantly in agreement despite my need to support Raine. "Fine. Two days. Then we'll come in."

He juts out his sharp jaw in acceptance, and I breathe a sigh of relief, grateful I could at least do something helpful. *Maybe I can also find some clues to share with Raphael and see if he can help protect Raine in return.*

Alaric turns to walk back to his car, but I call out to him. "Hey! Wait!" When he looks back, I grin. "Think you can give us a ride back to my place, and maybe call in a little snack for us too?"

A dark chuckle slips from him, but he stops himself abruptly, a look of shock lighting his features.

Maybe it's been a while since he laughed?

After the silence almost becomes awkward, he waves us forward, pulls out his cell phone, and begins tapping away. Hopefully sorting out some blood to be delivered to my place.

I turn back to Raine and take her hand to lead her over to the car.

"Come on. Let's go back to my place and we can talk. I promise he'll take us there—I can guarantee you, he will keep his word. I've known him for... a long time. Okay?"

Raine doesn't say anything, but she does start walking towards the car. I jump into the back seat with her and sit in silence as Alaric takes us back to my home.

I don't realize until much later that he never asked for the address.

BARGAIN

As Raine and I reach my apartment door, I see a small cooler and relief washes over me. Alaric has come through for my new houseguest—a nice surprise. I pick it up and unlock the door, gesturing for Raine to go in first.

She wanders past me, hand still on her throat, though thankfully with a blood-free face since there were wet wipes in Alaric's truck. He mentioned he always ended up with weird substances on him in his line of work. He even said it with a slight smile, which I couldn't help but return.

"Just take a seat on the couch over there," I say as I point toward the pair of gray two-seaters, sitting parallel on either side of my coffee table.

She walks over without a word and takes a seat. I head into the kitchen for one of my cute cat mugs, hoping Raine also likes them, and then sit opposite her. I carefully place the mug and cooler on the table.

"I know things have been scary. How are you doing?"

Her eyes well immediately, but she holds in the tears. "I'm better here than in that cemetery, but I really don't understand what's going on and why my throat hurts so much. I feel so... hungry? Or... or... thirsty, maybe?"

I lock my gaze on hers and keep a calm tone. "I know this is going to be hard to believe, and you're probably going to think I'm crazy, but try to stay with me, okay?" She nods at me to continue. "You've probably spent your whole life believing there are only humans on Earth, but there are more than just humans. Even though you don't know about them or see them, there are also supernatural beings here as well."

Raine's eyes bulge with a look of half incredulity and half fear. "You mean, like, aliens or something?"

I shake my head, forcing my lips to stay where they are, positive she won't appreciate my chuckle. "No, not aliens. More like things you've probably heard about in storybooks. Werewolves, shapeshifters, fae, angels, demons... vampires."

I look at her meaningfully, wondering if mentioning vampires might jog her memory, but it doesn't appear to do so.

Her expression becomes a little concerned. "Are you all right? Do *you* need help maybe?"

Regretfully, I shake my head, knowing she likely won't believe this without proof, but I try to add a little more information for her first.

"I'm okay, Raine, thank you. Like I said, I know this sounds a little wild at the moment. But you mentioned to me earlier that you were attacked after your date?"

I raise my eyebrows and wait for her to answer.

After a moment of fleeting emotions crossing her face, she says, "Yes."

"You were attacked by a master vampire."

Her hand slides to the side of her neck where slight bumps lay healed from her master's fangs. Fear floods her. I nod slowly, keeping eye contact in the hopes she won't bolt.

"You've been turned into a vampire as well. The reason your throat hurts so much is because you're thirsty."

She jumps up and I rise with her, sympathy coming from every pore. "Please," I say, "you're going to be okay. Just sit and I'll explain as best I can, all right?"

I watch as she runs her hands over her own body and licks her teeth. When she doesn't find any fangs, the tension drops from her muscles. "This isn't true. I don't have pointy teeth or whatever."

Deciding that sometimes showing is better than telling, I open the cooler and pull out a couple of the bags of blood. Before I can even get them to the table, Raine darts forward with supernatural speed and snatches the bags from me. Her fangs have dropped down and she uses them to pierce the bag, sucking out the blood without a word. Her eyes are red and crazed.

I stay still so she doesn't become defensive and let her finish, ignoring the blood she gets on herself and the specks that fly onto the table in front of her. She devours three more bags before her eyes begin to clear.

I see the moment she comes back to herself, blanching as she really looks at what she's holding and drinking. She drops the bag to the table, and I hurry to pick it up before the last bit spills. Raine immediately pulls her knees up to her chest on one of my couches and tears fall freely again.

"I'm a monster," she sobs. "Why did this happen to me? Can it be undone?" she adds, hopelessness dulling her tone.

"I'm sorry. You can't be changed back, but you're not a monster. What was done to you rarely ever happens like that anymore, and the one who did it will be in a huge amount of trouble. There are a lot of rules for supernaturals to help keep us and humans safe."

Her head bobs up and down, latching onto something she might be able to control in the chaos right now. "Rules. I can learn the rules. I'm good with those. Can you tell me? Will someone else tell me? Wait. Who was that guy who dropped us off from the cemetery? Is he a vampire? Are you?"

"Hey, it's all right. Just breathe. There will be plenty of time for questions. We can take this slow, okay? The main things you need to know are that we can't expose ourselves, or any other supernaturals, to humans, and that all supernatural groups have a council of their own, as well as one overall council to make sure we all remain hidden. That's called the Council of the Accord. Once we check you in with them, you'll get all the rules that you could ever need." Then I add wryly, "And probably some you don't."

"Right," she mutters. "And you and that guy—are you vampires too?"

"No. I'm half angel and half demon, and Alaric, the guy from the car, is a werewolf. He's also a Council enforcer, one of the supes who make sure we all follow the rules."

She shivers. "What was he going to do with me if he took me away?"

I purse my lips. "I don't know. Question you at the very least. But I will reach out to one of the angels on the Council of the Accord and see what we can do to sort this out. It's not like you asked to be turned, and you haven't hurt anyone."

"Oh, God. I might hurt someone!" She leans forward and grabs my forearms, squeezing them in desperation. "Please! You have to help me. I don't want to hurt anyone!"

I grimace in pain. "Raine, it's all right. I'll help you. Do you think you could loosen your grip a little? You're quite strong right now since you've just turned."

She gasps as she lets go. "I'm so sorry. Sorry."

"I'm okay. Really. It was just getting a little tight is all." I look over her dirt- and blood-stained clothes. She's probably around the same size as me. "How about you take a shower, and I'll get you some clean clothes, and we can go from there?"

Raine looks down and wrinkles her nose in distaste. "Uh, yes, please. Which way?"

I lead her down to the bathroom, then find some clothes, and set them outside the door before heading back to hunt down my phone. I stare at it, wondering how I'm going to contact Raphael, when it starts ringing.

"I believe you have an update for me, daughter of Estelle."

My brain throws on the brakes. "Raphael?"

"Indeed. Your news?"

"Right. Um. Well, I found my other client, Sophie, but she was staked."

He's silent for a moment, then speaks with more softness in his voice. "Yes. I did hear of Orpheus's decree. I am sorry. I can hear she meant much to you."

"Thank you," I say, touched that he seems to care despite his age and his unwillingness to get close to or show care for anyone—according to my mother. "The vampire has also turned someone else. A woman this time. A vision showed me where she would be, so I believe I was meant to find her. I have her with me. I don't want anything to happen to her."

Raphael's tone returns to his well-practiced neutrality. "I can arrange a meeting with the Council for you both to attend, but this is not a decision I can make on my own—not when she is a vampire. I believe addressing the Council will be the best chance you have for what you seek. Bring her the day after tomorrow. I will have blood arranged until then." As an afterthought, he adds, "Have you any idea of who the master vampire is yet?"

Astounded that he is being so helpful, I'm slow to speak. "I, um, thank you. For Raine. I'll bring her in then. As for the master, I don't know anything, but I'll try to ask Raine if she can remember anything once she's a little more rested."

"Very well. I shall call for another update if one arises. Farewell, Everleigh."

I open my mouth to answer but he's already gone. I pull the phone down from my ear and stare at it in disbelief.

How in the hells did he know to call me right then?

Raine comes back into the room with a mild smile lighting her features. "It sounded like pretty good news."

Raine and I sit in the hallway outside the Council meeting room, and she taps her fingers anxiously on the chair. It feels like déjà vu when I open my mouth to talk to her.

"Just remember: let me do the talking in there, okay? Unless they address you about something in particular."

She grimaces and nods. "Yes, I remember. I'm just nervous. Kind of life and death here, you know? Or un-death? Re-death? Ugh. You know what I mean."

"I know. It'll be okay. I'm hopeful I can convince them. You haven't done anything wrong. You've stayed with me, and it's all been fine."

We both look up when the elevator dings. Alaric walks out of the doors and heads straight for us, his tightly fitting clothes and chiseled jawline drawing my attention. *If only his words were as delightful as his looks.*

I wouldn't say no if he was on offer. Biting him into submission would be fun.

He tries to talk but the Council door opens, and he turns immediately towards it, leaving whatever he planned to say for later. This time, a young demon walks out to greet us, a lascivious smirk resting on his face. His eyes wander straight over Alaric and me, and then rest on Raine. He saunters towards her, his black leather clothes hugging every line and bulge—he looks like a model from a magazine, if the Hells had magazines anyway.

Seeing Raine step back, clearly unsure of the advance, I step directly in his way, stopping him in his tracks. Red flashes across his irises and a snarl pulls one corner of his mouth up.

Horny prat.

Stab him.

"Are you here to escort us in?" I ask in a bland voice, ignoring his childish behavior and the unhelpful suggestion of my inner demonic side. Clearly, Nicon wanted some eye candy. The demon in front of us isn't good for much more if this is the way he behaves while on duty.

When he doesn't speak and continues to stare, his eyes building to a solid red, I've had enough. I unleash the anger and pain that have been building inside me over the recent deaths of my clients and match my iris color to his.

"I suggest you get out of the way before I *move* you out of the way."

Before he can say another word, a ball of hellish blue fire encapsulates him from behind, and his screech pierces the air before he and the fire disappear. Raine gives a little shriek of terror while I lock eyes with the demon who just walked through the entrance door, clearly wondering what was taking so long.

Nicon.

He offers me a lusty smirk as his eyes roam over my body. "Shame about that. He was good to look at. Come on in. We've waited long enough."

He's such an enigma that I shake my head, and then look back to help Raine. "It's okay. He's just been moved back to his realm of the Hells for now. He's not dead or anything."

"Yeah. Right. Fine." Her head moves back and forth quickly, as though she doesn't notice she's doing it, and my heart aches for her. Transitioning to the supernatural world is hard enough without a baptism of fire.

"Come on. Let's get this over with."

Inside the room, Raine gets her first full taste of the supernatural species in our world, and since Nicon's assistant went up in smoke, the Council members introduce themselves.

In the moment of silence following their introductions, I step forward.

"I would like to introduce Raine Pillari." I gesture to her, and she bows like I showed her before we arrived. "She's the latest victim of the master vampire turning humans illegally."

Orpheus sits straighter in his chair. "How and why is it that you are the one making this introduction?" He spears his gaze to Alaric. "Why is it that an introduction is being made at all?"

To Alaric's credit, he doesn't back down from the poison spitting from the Vampire King's tone. Instead, he simply gestures back to me and waits expectantly for me to explain. I catch Raphael's gaze, and he gives me an almost imperceptible bow of his head, so I keep talking.

"I've been having visions of the humans who've been turned recently. I've attempted to use this information to track them in the hopes of saving them before they cause any damage, which I'm sure they would not be doing if they'd been given a proper introduction to our world. Sadly, I wasn't able to—" I clear my throat, trying to keep my tears at bay, so I can keep talking "—I wasn't able to save my former client, Sophie, who was one of the vampires previously turned. However, I was able to get to Raine before she hurt herself or anyone else."

"That is not your job," Orpheus grinds out. "You are not an enforcer, and you are definitely not at liberty to decide what happens to newly turned vampires. Especially ones made without approval."

"Oh, Orphy," Iridessa purrs, twirling a strand of her ruby hair. "Anyone would think you're losing control. Surely one teeny, baby vampire isn't going to be any problem?" She smiles prettily at him, the picture of innocence despite her provocative choice of words.

I do my best to keep my disbelief off my face, especially since she seems to be on my side this time.

Raphael clears his throat to gain everyone's attention. "While I understand your concerns, Orpheus, I don't see any harm in fully inducting Raine into our world given she has caused no harm despite being turned several days ago. I believe Everleigh has done a fine job keeping Raine's thirst under control through regular blood deliveries, and Raine has stayed away from the humans."

The Council murmurs their agreement with the exception of Solomon, who remains silent. Not willing to object when the majority has spoken but not agreeing with them either. Not that it really matters to me as long as Raine gets to live.

Iridessa taps her sharp nails on her small table, drawing the attention of the room back to her, though now she's staring at me. "Miss Cole, it seems you get your wish once more with the Council, though I think some compensation might be due. What are you willing to give to continue taking Miss Pillari under your wing, so to speak? Or will you be handing her off to the vampire council to manage?"

Orpheus bursts up from his seat. "You cannot decide that! You have no right to make such an arrangement."

Iridessa doesn't bother looking at the Vampire King. She simply stares at me with one side of her lips curved up and a delicate brow raised in question.

Octavia looks at me with concern and what appears to be regret. "I'm afraid I have to agree with Orpheus on this front. We do not make such decisions. Unless..." She pauses and looks from me to Raphael and back again. "Unless there is something Miss Cole might be able to offer in return for this amendment?"

I ignore the churning in my gut and briefly look at Raine. She appears terrified. I suppose I would too if I was just told I'd be sent off to be dealt with by an entire vampire council. I give her a reassuring smile before addressing the room.

"I understand that vampires are typically the responsibility of the vampire council, and I would be willing to offer a trade to keep Raine with me during her initial transition period."

Octavia nods for me to continue.

"In exchange for Raine staying with me rather than being handed off to the vampire council, I would be willing to use my visions to help with this case, to assist in tracking down the master vampire illegally turning people."

Solomon objects immediately, voice smug. "We do not need some random hybrid helping with this case. We have enforcers for that."

Do all mages have their heads this far up their arses?

There's a pause before Raphael gives his opinion.

"Considering how many turned vampires and dead people we are now dealing with, and the increasing human awareness, I suggest we consider this option carefully. These case-related visions are already coming to Everleigh. We have little to no leads for our enforcers to follow. The situation is out of control."

Iridessa pipes up again, practically purring, "Oh, yes. I agree with Raphael, Orphy. Everleigh is the best lead we have so far. Surely one more vampire out of your control won't matter."

Orpheus looks like he wants to hack Iridessa's head off. And even though she's on my side, the way she is presenting her view of the case is definitely making things worse.

Octavia cuts into the conversation again, attempting to smooth things over, and drawing the Vampire King's attention from the Fae Queen. "Orpheus, this is a temporary situation for both the case and Miss Pillari. Having her stay with Everleigh while she helps on the case also means she will have easy access to your new vampire should she recall anything pertinent about her master."

I hear Alaric's mouth pop open, then slam shut at Octavia's comment. The expression on his face is clearly unhappy with the idea of a tag-a-long for this case.

If Orpheus's fangs weren't retracted, I'm sure in his anger he'd have snapped them off by now, but he seems to swallow it down to say, "Yes. It seems too good of an opportunity to pass up given the death toll we currently face." He looks at me. "I expect reports from you and Alaric if these visions occur, and you both are to attend the next vampire council meeting on Friday evening this week. Perhaps being in attendance will provide some clues, or perhaps even a vision to help things along. The master needs to be held accountable as soon as possible before others begin to develop such foolish ideas and spark a rebellion."

Ah. So he's worried about an uprising. I suppose letting me help Raine is a better alternative for him than that.

"Very well," Conall calls, gaining the attention of the Council for the first time this evening. He looks directly at Alaric and holds his gaze, leaving no room for disagreement. "You will include Everleigh in everything case-related and heed any suggestions she makes regarding this matter. You will remain responsible for reporting back on any progress made. Understood?"

"Yes, sir," Alaric says in his practiced monotone.

Conall nods, and Alaric turns and leaves the room immediately, evidently done with the conversation. His boldness impresses me. I definitely wouldn't leave without being dismissed. His king stares a hole in Alaric's back but makes no comment. Briefly, I hope he doesn't get into strife for that later, especially since it sounds like I'll be dealing with the emotional fallout.

When I turn to the side, I see Nicon offering me a salacious grin. "Well, I think that's all for today, ladies. It seems it's time for you both to leave."

"I thank the Council for their time and decision today," I say before bowing, then I take Raine's arm, and we leave the room.

Over the next few days, texts from Alaric mostly consist of asking me if I've had any visions and telling me whenever someone is murdered. In our short phone calls, he lets me know about several new vampires being turned—some found and put down, and some turned over to the vampire council if they were caught early enough.

I sit on the couch next to Raine, watching an old action movie with plenty of death and destruction. A way to channel some of my anger and frustration with the situation. I try my best to tell Raine everything she wants to know about the supernatural world without showing too much of myself and trying not to find out excessive amounts about her life. People who get close to me seem to get punished or killed, and I'm not ready to get close enough to be hurt like that again. The problem is that Raine is sweet and kind, and finding out she was a teacher of young children just makes so much sense.

Despite my best efforts, she seems to be inching her way into my heart.

"Everleigh, are you okay?" she asks with a gentle lull to her tone.

"What? Oh, sorry, yes. I'm fine. Just preoccupied with the case and the Council meeting tomorrow night."

She gives me a sympathetic look. "You still aren't getting any visions?"

I shake my head. "I don't know why but I haven't gotten any since I found you."

She flinches at my words, and I hurry to clarify, sharing a little more information about myself. "Angel visions seem to work based on some kind of motivation I don't understand. From my experience, I'd say whatever guiding light directs me, *wanted* me to find you, but there isn't anything it wants to direct my attention toward right now." I add dryly, "I have no doubt when there is something my guide wants me to know, I'll find out."

Raine relaxes against the couch after I explain what I mean, and I can't help feeling much the same. I don't want her to believe it's her fault. There's enough happening for her, though the ease of her transition surprises me.

"You know, your transition is going really well. Considering how recently you were turned, you seem to be managing the blood cravings and keeping a clear head more effectively than other recently turned vampires I've met."

A very slight pink color reaches her cheeks, and she grins at me, appearing—for better or worse—as though she looks up to me. "That's because you've been such a great teacher. And I've honestly been so well fed that cravings haven't been a problem for me at all."

"I'm not sure you're giving yourself enough credit, but thank you. I'm doing my best to make this as smooth as possible for you."

"You know, you're just so kind, Everleigh. I haven't actually met anyone who has cared as much as you since I lost my parents ten years ago."

I frown, sadness blossoming. "I'm sorry to hear they've passed. What happened?"

Raine gives me a sad smile. "They were killed by a drunk driver. The guy came flying around a corner, speeding massively, crossed onto their side of the road, and hit them head-on. They died instantly. They were the nicest people. Always helping others, putting neighbors and strangers first. If they were here, I don't even think they'd be mad about it. And they wouldn't want me to be mad about what's happened to me either. Mom and Dad would just want me to make the best of this situation and keep on helping others."

Despite the tragedy in her life, her soul still manages to shine through, and I feel my eyes take on their golden warmth in response to the genuineness she shares with me. "I have no doubt they're proud of you, Raine. I know I am."

As we return to a more companionable silence while watching the television, I can't help the thawing in my heart, and I wonder if it's going to make me stronger or be the thing that gets me killed.

WATCHED

MY DOORBELL BUZZES, AND I rush out of my bedroom while still pulling on a shirt. "Just a second!"

I open the door halfway and freeze for a split second. *What is the High Witch doing in my doorway?* "Miss Witt. To what do I owe the pleasure?"

"Octavia will be fine, thank you, Everleigh. I am actually here to see both yourself and Raine if that is all right?" Her brows rise slightly in question as she looks past me towards the living room.

Caught somewhere between respecting the hierarchy of the supernatural world and protecting Raine, I take longer than is probably polite to gesture for her to come in. *I hope her taking my side on the Council vote means she's safe enough to invite in.*

She keeps her calm demeanor and walks straight towards the lounge chair.

"I'll fetch Raine, but can I get you something to drink before I do that?" I ask.

Octavia smiles slightly. "I'm quite all right, though I thank you for offering."

"Of course," I murmur and head down the hall.

Raine's bedroom door is open, but her back is to me. Headphones are over her ears with music so loud, I can hear the classical piano tune from here. I walk closer and see her sketching a scene of small children.

As I get closer, she pulls her headphones off, hitting Pause on the new smartphone we bought for her yesterday. "What's going on?"

"Octavia Witt, the High Witch from the Council of the Accord, is here. She wants to see us both."

Raine raises one arched eyebrow at me, and I simply shrug, not sure what to tell her. *It's not like we really have a choice.*

The High Witch stands when we return to the room, her deep gray ringlets bouncing gently against the shoulders of her gray-blue cloak. "Raine, it's lovely to see you looking so well."

The smile Raine returns to Octavia is one of genuine happiness, and I wonder at the odds of me finding such a kind supe to take in, when my vision could have easily chosen any of the others.

"It's nice to see you as well. What brings you here?" Raine asks the older lady with a hint of nerves.

I gesture for everyone to take seats, then look expectantly at the witch, curious to hear her answer myself.

Octavia pulls a small box from inside her cloak and opens the lid before turning it around and presenting it to Raine. I smile, realizing the answer to our question immediately.

Raine gasps, clutching one hand to her heart and the other to her mouth. "It's stunning," she breathes. "Is that really for me? Why are you giving me something so exquisite?"

Octavia bows her head slightly at the younger woman's response. "The rose-shaped stone on this necklace is a lapis lazuli. Each vampire, upon their creation and registration, has a stone crafted into a piece of jewelry. Witches imbue it with magical protections, and together, they allow you to walk in the sun without being burned or harmed. I saw to the creation of this one myself, given the special circumstances."

I grin at Octavia, both surprised and heartened by her efforts for the young vampire, especially when Raine had such a poor reception from her own kind—though I understand from experience that there are those always willing to hate anything different.

"I—" Raine takes a deep breath, pulls a tissue from her pocket, and wipes the bloodied tears that spill from her eyes. "Thank you. Truly. I thought I would never get to go outside and feel the sun's warmth again. What a precious gift. And it's so beautifully crafted as well."

Guilt weighs down my chest as soon as she shares her gratitude with Octavia. I realize with everything going on with her, Henry, and Alaric, I had completely forgotten to tell Raine about needing a stone. I don't want to interrupt the moment she is having now, but I make a commitment to apologize to her later for the oversight and for not following up with the Council sooner.

Raine places the necklace over her head, the delicate gold chain long enough that the stone falls below the line of her shirt, certain to keep it hidden from prying eyes. She runs her fingers over it gently, hope lighting her features.

"Just a note of warning," Octavia adds. "Each vampire is only ever gifted *one* of these stones. They are difficult to make and getting another will be next to impossible. Take very good care of your necklace."

Raine nods seriously but earnestly at the witch's words. "Of course. I'll take very good care of it."

"Very well," she says before turning her attention to me. "Now, I understand you are to attend the vampire council meeting this evening with Alaric to attempt to get more information. Is that still the case?"

"Yes. Alaric texted last night to confirm. He's going to collect me from here so he can brief me in the car."

"Very well. I'm fairly certain you have not attended such an event before?"

"That's right. I've tended to... keep my distance in the past."

"Yes, I understand. I want to leave you with a warning. I am sure you are well versed in vampire lore and the like but given Orpheus's attempt to enthrall you at the Council meeting the day you met, I thought it best I say something anyway. Avoid eye contact with those in the room. It is highly unlikely that any other would have enough power if Orpheus does not, but if it should happen to work, it would make you very vulnerable to their suggestion and solving this case may become impossible.

Especially if, as I suspect, the master vampire responsible may be present."

I sit straighter. "Thank you for the warning. Why is it you think the one responsible will be at the meeting?"

"The... *audacity* of someone illegally turning humans in this city despite the presence of the entire Council speaks of great power to me. Over my years in this position, I have observed power and age clash many times to the detriment of the innocents around us. This blatant disregard reminds me of such a thing. I have no proof but felt you were worthy of a warning, given the risk you take going into such a situation and trying to trigger a vision to solve this case."

"That's very kind of you. I didn't know I'd done anything to warrant such respect from someone such as yourself, Octavia." I stand tall, trying to show my respect and worthiness in her presence.

"Au contraire, you have, Everleigh. Not many will risk their life for the lives of humans or those they don't know. Especially supes with very extended lifespans. If there is help that I can give without causing any major issues among the species, I shall endeavor to do so."

I nod, stunned and warmed by Octavia's admission. My relationships with supernaturals seem to be erring on the side of positivity these days, and the fluttering wings in my stomach tell me I'm a little unsure about how to deal with it.

"Thank you, your kind words and actions are well received and appreciated."

She inclines her head, shocking me once again, and heat rises to my cheeks. Having so much respect and care shown by supes feels so unnatural to me that I'm not sure how to process the information. Instead, I file it away for later and return her bow.

Octavia makes her way to the door, but as she reaches the threshold, a dark feeling builds in my gut. My mind immediately pulls towards Raine, and I heed the instinct, thinking quickly on my feet. "Excuse me, Octavia?"

She turns back with a curious gaze. "Yes?"

My brows draw down as I consider the best way to phrase my request. I decide on honesty. "I'm not sure of the right way to ask, but I'm getting a bad feeling about the threshold here. I wondered if you might add a layer of protection to it on your way out?"

Octavia's expression turns serious. "Of course. That is easy enough for me to do. Stay inside and close the door. I'll add a ward." She steps through and turns to look back at us. "I suggest you avoid opening the door for a good fifteen minutes to give it sufficient time to settle in the surrounding walls and windows. If anything else comes to you, reach out to the Council."

I bow from the hips in a show of thanks and respect, knowing fully she could choose not to add her protection, especially when neither Raine nor I are of her species and therefore not her responsibility to protect.

She meets my eyes momentarily, then pulls the door shut. I hear her muttering and feel the pull of magic being laid. The presence feels strong, powerful, and solid. The foreboding in my stomach dissipates a little, and the drop in intensity allows me to breathe a little easier.

I turn to Raine, finding it possible to offer a reassuring smile with Octavia's protection in place. "Come on. Let's go watch a show you enjoy before I have to go out tonight. I picked last night."

She returns my smile, electing not to speak the fears hiding in her eyes, willing for now to follow my lead. She runs her finger over her new necklace beneath her shirt, and then leads the way to the sofa and television. When she sits, she turns to me, her voice taking on a mischievous tone. "I know just what to pick."

A couple of sexy, funny movies later, and I feel lighter. Bantering with Raine is too easy, and I'm so enthralled by her tales of teaching young children and the hilarious things they say, that I startle when loud knocks hit my front door. I look at the time on my watch. "Oh, crap! That's Alaric."

Raine laughs lightly as I rush to answer the door before he decides to break it down.

I yank it open and am confronted with Alaric's steely gaze.

"Sorry. Sorry! I lost track of time. Come in. Just give me a second." I gesture towards the lounge chair and then hurry off to my bedroom. "Oh. And close the door!" I call out to him.

I quickly pull on dark jeans, wedge-heeled black leather boots, and a dark turtleneck top—no need to tease the vamps. I glance at my outfit and decide Clara would approve. I look kind of badass right now. Amused, I shake my head and pull my hair into a single plait before rushing back to join Alaric and Raine.

I suck in my cheeks to try and hold back a smile, knowing Alaric won't thank me for it. Raine has somehow got him talking about small insignificant things, a feat I was fairly sure was impossible. His façade is usually as hard as the eight-pack of abs I saw him sporting in Paris.

When he sees me, he stops mid-sentence, nods at Raine, and returns to the door to leave.

Raine rushes over to me and gives me a hug. I freeze, surprised at the sudden show of affection, then lean into her and squeeze her back.

"Stay in tonight, okay?"

"Of course," she says. "You stay safe as well. I'll see you again when it's over?"

"You can count on it," I say, relieved when my gut doesn't indicate otherwise. I turn and follow Alaric outside, making sure to lock the door behind me.

I roll my eyes when we pull up at the vampire council's meeting location. It's an obscenely large and swanky-looking mansion that belongs to one of them with more money than sense. How they got Council approval for something so showy is beyond me. When we get out, I see an actual red carpet running from the doorway to the driveway and let out an indelicate snort.

"Ridiculous, isn't it?" Alaric mutters.

"Yeah, something like that. Who lives here?"

"Orpheus."

"Ah," I say. "Well, that makes sense."

I walk to the front door ahead of Alaric, which is guarded by two bored-looking male vamps. I feel eyes staring, and I whip my head around. Alaric's eyes fling up and meet mine briefly before he looks away, the faintest pink tinging his chiseled face. Slightly shocked, but secretly a little pleased, I continue up the staircase.

"Gentlemen," I say. "We're here for the council meeting."

The one on my right nods to his sharply dressed counterpart. They open the doors simultaneously and avoid eye contact as Alaric and I pass. Inside, the house is just as lavish as the outside, except instead of the typical, white-colored walls, these are charcoal gray. Large paintings in deep mahogany frames line the walls. I raise a single eyebrow at Alaric. He shrugs, appearing completely nonplussed by the décor.

A female vampire, draped in a deep-crimson dress that looks like it could be worth a month of my human job's paycheck, walks towards us from the far end of the hall. Her dark hair is braided in a single plait, which sits over her left shoulder and ends at her hips, and she grins with her fangs out. "Welcome to Master Orpheus's home. I have been sent to collect you so that the discussion you are here for might begin. This way, please." She waves a hand toward the direction from which she came and then turns and heads back the same way.

This time, Alaric takes the lead and I follow behind, taking the opportunity to check out *his* tight ass in his jeans.

Once we reach a set of heavy timber doors, our vampire escort knocks several times and then leads us into the meeting. The room is set up like a miniature coliseum, with the vampire council sitting in raised stands and Orpheus alone in a booth, perched on what appears to be a throne. And us? We're on the floor in the center. *Very subtle.*

"Welcome, Alaric Bane and Everleigh Cole, to the vampire council meeting. Very few outsiders are granted entrance here," Orpheus states from his seat.

Another male vampire, who looks a few years older than Orpheus's thirtyish appearance, stands. "And why exactly are they here?" he demands. Upon seeing the feral look flash across the Vampire King's face, he tacks on, "Your Greatness."

"As I was about to say, Aldair, these guests are here as... enforcers for the Council, investigating the recently turned vampires for which no approval was granted." Orpheus looks down at Alaric. "You may present the case as it stands and we shall proceed from there."

While Alaric briefs the council of vampires on the bare minimum of information, including the number of dead or missing humans in the area, the suspected number of newly turned progeny, and the request for feedback from the members in attendance today, I watch the crowd. The expressions vary as much as those present, some showing nothing, some haunted with fear, others disgusted at the blatant disregard for the rules and customs that keep them safe from human exposure. And a select few who look amused.

I do my best to document them all in my mind.

When he finishes speaking, Alaric turns back to Orpheus and waits silently.

The Vampire King stands and addresses his council. "Right. The case to date has been outlined. You may now elect to speak on behalf of your covens if you so choose." He sits back on his throne and observes the rest of the council, some raise their hands, and he takes a long moment before announcing who will talk first.

"Morgana," he says.

The vampire in question stands to address everyone. "I have not had any deaths or disappearances within my coven's boundaries at this point, though I imagine that is not going to do much to rule us out. Do you wish for us to interrogate our own coven members?"

Her expression is both displeased and resigned, accepting that she will do what is required of her.

Alaric responds before Orpheus has a chance to do so. "On behalf of the enforcers, I would ask that no interrogations be enacted at this stage of the investigation. If such an approach is needed, we will discuss the situation with King Orpheus ahead of time."

With some relief, Morgana nods and takes her seat.

With loosely disguised disdain, Orpheus gestures to another vampire to speak. "Elias."

The vamp stands with an amused sneer. "Well, it sounds as though your investigation is going a whole lot of nowhere. Perhaps it's time we take matters into our own hands."

Murmuring starts among the council, and I try to keep track of the members, though it's hard when they're in a circle above us.

Another male vampire stands, one with little expression and a quieter voice. "I see no sense in causing chaos among the clans beyond what is happening in this room. I am sure, between King Orpheus and the enforcers, this will be resolved in due time."

Orpheus nods. "Thank you, Silas. A wise response as always."

Silas offers a bow, and sits once more, his expression remaining neutral.

"Louisa."

"I agree with Elias insofar as needing to deal with this issue in house. Surely this is a vampire problem?"

The majority of the council members stand and give their opinions, and I see Alaric watching and listening as intently as I do, perhaps taking note of who he thinks warrants more investigation.

After what feels like several hours of going in circles, Orpheus stands and draws the attention of the room. "After listening to the opinions of the council, it seems we are almost evenly split, and thus I will make a decision at this time—pending review. We shall leave this to the enforcers to deal with for the present time, and I expect full cooperation from anyone to whom they wish to speak on pain of death if you refuse."

He eyes Elias among the council, who glares back at him, lips pinched tight. Orpheus then looks down to us. "We thank you for your efforts, and I would appreciate an update as soon as you have one. For now, please excuse us so that we may move on to hors d'oeuvres."

The dark-haired vampire in the dress behind us opens the doors for us to leave. One step towards the door and my vision begins to lighten, my steps falter, and I hold out a hand to steady myself, not familiar enough with the space to grab onto anything. After half a second, I feel a hot, muscled forearm under my hand. I utter an internal sigh of relief and let Alaric guide me out the door, unable to hold the vision back any longer.

Darkness. An office of sorts. Lit only by moonlight.

Old tomes. Ancient trinkets. A desk with a glass of blood and a darkened wine bottle.

A growl. Male. Items thrown and smashed against a wall. A glass shattered.

Halfway down the hall my sight is back, and despite my heart racing, I pull my lips up into a grin as I realize our presence in the council meeting has been successful—we've forced a reaction from whoever is behind all of this.

To—mostly—avoid causing a scene, I keep my hand linked with Alaric's arm until we are out the doors and down the stairs. Once we're back in the car, he turns on the engine and speeds away, impatient to know what I do. After we get to a safe distance, he slows the car and glances at me.

"Did you get something?" he asks.

I smile. "Not an exact answer, but we definitely made a splash. I'm willing to bet it was one of the men in that room. From the looks of the items in the office he was smashing, I'd say he's been turned for a very long time and has a lot of money."

Alaric nods, some of the tension leaving his shoulders. "Good. Now we wait for the ripples."

I switch on my phone and it dings several times with missed calls and texts.

Raine: Someone's trying to get in!

Raine: When will you be back?

Raine: Please hurry. They're trying all the entrances!

"Shit! Step on it, Alaric. Someone's trying to break into my apartment to get to Raine!"

PROTECTED

As soon as Alaric pulls up to the front of my apartment building, I jump straight out of the car while cursing the need to hide from the humans and race up the stairs to the third floor.

Thank goodness the wards held.

Trying not to cause alarm to the rest of the building, lest we end up with the police here, I unlock the door and push it open.

"Argh!" My heart skids to a halt as I jump back from the fire poker that jabs out towards my chest.

"Sorry. Sorry! Are you okay?"

My heart begins to slow as I huff out a breath. "I'm okay. It's all right. Are you okay?"

Raine nods as Alaric runs up the final flight of stairs towards us after parking the car, fury lighting his frosty gaze.

"Let's get inside," I say, ushering them both in and closing the door.

"I'm sorry about all the calls and texts. The wards held, but I could see someone trying to gain access through the fire escape, the windows on both sides, and the front door. I didn't know what else to do."

I open my mouth to speak but Alaric cuts me off. "Did you see them?"

I glare at him for making this about the case instead of Raine when she's clearly distressed.

She shuffles her feet and glances at the floor. "All I can tell you is that it was a guy dressed in a suit."

I sigh, grumpy with myself for not knowing anyone in the supe community well enough that I can call and ask them to watch over Raine. But pissed off too, because I allowed myself to push the worry from my mind after getting Octavia to cast the wards.

"It's probably got to do with this case," I say. "We shook up whoever is responsible for all of this, but I didn't think anything would come from it so quickly. Did the man trying to get in look familiar? Could it have been the one who changed you?" I ask gently.

She shakes her head and looks between me and Alaric as she says, "I'm sorry, I really can't remember much about when I was turned. I was attacked from behind. He did smell like an old musk, and had strong hands, but I guess he's a vampire so that part doesn't tell us much. Since I didn't see him, I don't know if it's the same vamp or not."

"It's not your fault, Raine." I turn to Alaric. "Maybe some local CCTV footage could help. I think the building has cameras if you can get someone from the office to investigate it?"

He nods, his eyes like a dark storm, and stands. "Let's call it a night. Ring me if you see anything else."

By the time Saturday morning rolls around, I haven't had any visions and Alaric hasn't sent any messages. I've taken some personal leave so I can stay close to Raine, and the both of us are going stir-crazy sitting at home.

The doorbell buzzes, and I jump up, making sure Raine heads off to her bedroom before I open it.

"Henry! How are you? Come in."

Henry smiles, just like always, and some of the tension leaves me. He wanders in, hugging me on the way through.

"Hey, Ev. I'm doing good. Getting some more sleep finally. I've been missing you at work, though. Is everything okay?"

Heat rises in my cheeks. "Yes, sorry, Henry. I really should have called, but things have been a little crazy." I close the door and follow him to the couch, where he's already making himself comfortable. "I do actually have a... friend here. I'd like to introduce you. She's lovely, but she is a vampire, so it's totally all right if you don't feel up to it."

Henry's smile falters for a moment, then comes back even stronger. "I'd like to meet your friend. I've been reading a lot about vampires since I got all the information from the Council. And like you said, they don't usually behave like the one in the alley did."

I flinch, realizing he doesn't know about Sophie being the vamp who killed our other clients in the alley. Since it's not something he needs to know, I leave it. "That's really great, Henry. My friend's name is Raine. I'll invite her out."

I walk to the kitchen, grab a bag of blood for Raine, then head down to her room. "Hey, you remember my human friend from work I told you about?"

She looks at me uncertainly. "Yeah. I remember. Is that him who came inside? I can smell him."

"It is, and I wondered, if after a bag of blood"—I hand it to her—"you'd like to meet him?"

She pinches her lips together for a moment. "Are you sure I'm ready?"

I smile warmly at her. "I'm sure, Raine. You've done so well, and honestly, I think if you were going to jump him, you would have already done it by now since you could scent him the moment he came through the door."

Her smile transforms her face, and she sits a little straighter before nodding. She quickly sucks down the contents of the bag and then looks up at me expectantly.

"Just remember to be gentle. You're extra strong since you've just been turned."

"Oh, yes. Of course." She jumps up from her desk, leaving her art pencils strewn across the surface. "Yay! I get to meet my first human... as, you know, a not-human!"

She looks as though she's being given a long-awaited gift, and her joy is contagious, a sharp relief to the stress we've been feeling all week. I let her lead the way out, almost bouncing in her excitement.

Raine sees Henry lounging on the couch, and she pauses briefly before she turns back to me and whispers, "You didn't say he was so scrumptious looking!"

Laughter breaks free from deep inside me. "I suppose I didn't. He's been a friend since I moved here and is a human. I try not to pay too much attention in that department."

She shrugs and continues on her way. Henry sees her and grins so big, both of his dimples show.

"Hi," he says. "I'm Henry."

"Raine," she answers quickly.

When she gets close enough, they have an awkward moment about whether to shake hands or hug, and eventually settle on a brief hug. I watch, laughter bubbling in my chest, as Raine barely touches him, clearly trying to be gentle.

I sit quietly, listening with interest as Henry tells Raine all about the things he has learned since discovering the existence of our world. Raine is loving every piece of information he shares, stopping him regularly to ask questions. Occasionally they ask me something, and I try to give them information without oversharing details that might piss someone off.

My phone chimes with a text notification and I eagerly tap to open it.

Alaric: I've got a lead on the one who tried to break in. Coming?

Me: Really?

Alaric: Be there in 10.

My heart starts racing, a mix of excitement and anxiety.

"Is everything okay, Ev?" Henry asks.

"Oh, yeah. Sorry, I need to step out soon, but I'll be back as quickly as I can."

I pause, unsure what to do about the two of them, when Henry steps in.

"I need to head off, too, but Raine, I could give you my number so we can keep chatting about this later if you want?"

"That would be great!"

I slide into Alaric's car and instantly feel the heat of his gaze but try to play it cool. "Hey. Where are we heading?"

After a moment longer of his intense look, he answers, his voice huskier than usual. "To the edge of the city—one of those swanky neighborhoods we visited for the vampire council meeting. Some of the witches running tech tracked down the vamp who was trying to break in here. They were able to follow him after he left in a car." He pauses, then adds, "Buckle up."

An unexpected warmth blooms inside me at Alaric's sudden care for my safety and willingness to include me after the attempted break in. I pull the seat belt across my lap and click it into place. "Right. Ready to go."

After a few minutes of quiet driving, butterflies flutter about in my stomach. The silence in the car feels different, like Alaric is trying to think of something to say compared to his usual strategy of minimal engagement. I press my lips together and wait, curious if he will say anything that isn't about the case.

"There were several more deaths overnight," he says. "We think another vamp has been turned. Keeping this out of the news is getting harder for our people. If we don't solve this soon, I don't know what the Council will do to manage it. Tensions are getting higher."

A heaviness sits in my chest, both because of the news of more deaths, but also because he opted to speak about the case and not try to talk about anything else. "Yes. It's getting really bad. I might need to try something more proactive to initiate my visions if this doesn't pan out."

He takes his eyes off the road. "What do you mean 'initiate your visions'? You can *make* them happen?" His tone almost sounds angry and accusatory.

I sit a little straighter and stare right back at him. "Not in the way you think. If any angel could initiate any vision about anything, then they wouldn't have bothered assigning me to this case."

Alaric stiffens a little, then gruffly adds, "Right. Sorry. How does it work then?"

"Visions are usually given to us by some kind of higher power, like God or whatever, when they're relevant to our lives and we have the opportunity to intervene in some way. The details, naturally, we need to figure out ourselves. Most angels—you know, not the hybrid kind like me—get whole visions that show all the details they would need to help at the right time. Me, well..." I crinkle my nose. "Mine don't work like that. I just get snippets, which often miss important information that I need. But sometimes, if I can use the clues in those visions, I can try to initiate a vision off by repeating a certain sound or touching something or someone who might be involved. It doesn't always work, and I need enough of a clue to have a starting point, but... yeah. That's how it works for me."

He's quiet for long enough that I feel uncomfortable, and I start tapping my fingers on the door of the car. Knowing I'm defective compared to the other angels is bad enough, but admitting it out loud makes my stomach swirl, especially when Alaric doesn't answer right away.

I see him peek in my direction from my peripheral vision and I do my best to stop the tapping, a nervous habit I've picked up over the years.

"I'm sorry," he mutters. "It must be hard. Being so different, and having your powers not work like anyone else's."

I turn and lock eyes with him, raw emotion swelling in my chest and making me feel like my throat is going to close over. It's the most empathetic thing anyone has ever managed to say to me in the supernatural community and no words will come out.

Alaric clears his throat. "We're, uh, we're here. Are you ready?"

I rein my emotions back in and take a deep breath before offering him a hesitant smile. "Yeah. Let's go."

We get out and slam our doors shut at the exact same moment, and my vision flashes to white. *Great timing.*

A back alley. Darkness. Moaning. Sobs. Blood trickling to the concrete.

Fangs tearing. Ripping. A scream. Silence.

An old window. A man. Red, crazed eyes. Anger. Disgust.

"Everleigh?" A quiet, masculine voice. A warm grip on my shoulder, and a light squeeze. "Everleigh, are you with me?"

My normal vision comes back over the next few seconds, and I turn my head and look up into Alaric's stormy eyes, closer to mine than they've ever been. The flutters come back, and I can't help but drop my gaze to his lips before I remind myself of what I just saw and why we're here. *Come on, Everleigh, focus for goodness' sake!*

I rip my eyes away and take a step back, both relieved and disappointed when he steps away. "Yeah. Right. I'm good, sorry. Another vamp I haven't seen. Freshly turned. A youngish guy, twenties maybe. Another two dead." I cringe, and sigh, completely over seeing so many people lose their lives because of one supe's actions. "A couple, in an alley. I didn't see too much. Sorry."

He nods stiffly and pulls out his phone. He sends a message to someone, and then looks back at me. "Let's grab some stuff out of the trunk and get moving before we lose this guy. The tech team said his car is still here."

I follow him around to the trunk of the car and look at what he has inside. Silver nets, silver spray, wooden stakes, cuffs, a wooden crossbow, and some kind of curved knife I haven't seen before. I'm grateful he lets me just pick what I like, recalling our time in Paris where I had to prove to him that I could manage weapons. One thing my father made sure of before he left us to seek revenge on the demon who killed our mother was that we knew how to fight every species of supe.

Reaching into the trunk, I decide I'd rather not get too close if I can help it, so I grab the spray and reach for the crossbow, but as soon as I touch it, all I can see is Sophie's face, and emotion wells inside me until I feel like I might choke on it. I leave the crossbow and opt for one of the knives instead.

If Alaric notices, he doesn't say anything, but he doesn't grab the crossbow either. It feels like a weight lifts from me at not having to bring that along. He collects a pair of blades the same as mine, locking them into a belt, and then takes a couple of stakes. When we step back, he pushes a button, and we wait while the car takes its sweet time to close and click shut.

He reaches into the back seat, pulls out two leather jackets, and hands one to me. "It's big, but it's just to cover your gear while we walk around on the streets."

"Oh, yeah. I didn't think of that. Not exactly used to carrying weapons around the local streets."

He shrugs, somehow managing to look even hotter wearing the leather jacket he's just shucked on. "It's second nature for me now. Let's move."

I pull the jacket on and subtly inhale the masculine scent of woods and earth and fresh rain. A little shiver runs through me, and I pinch myself on the thigh in an effort to refocus.

I follow Alaric along the street, sticking close to the giant fences that prevent prying eyes from seeing into the houses. There are only a few cars on the street, mostly expensive models. Alaric comes to a halt in front of me, and I step into the heat radiating from his body and peer around him to get a better look.

We've reached a set of double gates with an intercom out the front. When I step around him, I can see the house. It's a standard two-story home that looks almost identical to the ones we've passed. Nothing really special about it, aside from the fact that it probably cost a couple million dollars. Still, the Council would approve of this—we're meant to blend in.

Alaric approaches the walk-in gate to the left of the driveway and does something I can't see, but it sounds like a muted version of metal being crushed. The gate swings open and I follow him through, trying to keep quiet because the vamp inside will likely hear us if we make much noise. We stick close to the giant hedges that line both sides of the driveway until they curve around to the front of the house.

Three cars are parked outside—expensive models like the ones on the street. Alaric huffs, sounding frustrated. He mutters to me, "They could have mentioned he had company when they tracked him."

I murmur my agreement but nudge him forward, my heart rate increasing as I anticipate the fight that is sure to come.

Alaric gives me a stern look and I roll my eyes, giving him an exaggerated "well, go on" gesture so that he'll get moving again. Instead of approaching the front of the house like I think he will, Alaric makes his way around the back. He was more of a knock-the-door-down kinda guy in Paris.

We break in through the back, and I'm grateful for the music they have playing, which we couldn't hear from outside the house, suggesting the vamp must have some kind of soundproofing in place. When we're almost in the same room as our guy and his friends, Alaric pauses at the same moment I remember I don't know what this vamp looks like. My lips curve up on my right side when Alaric pulls out his smartphone and shows me a picture of the one we're here for. He shouldn't be hard to miss—slim, bald head, sharp jaw, and a scar under his left eye. I nod, and Alaric silently puts his phone away.

My heart almost stops when Alaric proceeds straight into the room, uncaring of the noise he's making. We have the attention of three vamps immediately. The odds don't appear to be in our favor.

The three vamps stop what they're doing and stare right at us. The one we're here for doesn't say anything, but a flash of fear runs through his eyes, and he takes a step back.

"Now, now, Evan," Alaric says to our vamp. "Don't be running off. We need to have a talk with you."

One of the other vamps snarls. "Who in the hells are you, and what are you doing sneaking into Evan's house? It's against the Accord and you know it."

Alaric gives him an easy smirk and slides his jacket to the side, showing not only his enforcer badge, but also one of the stakes strapped to his belt. "I'm going to suggest that if your name isn't Evan, you leave now."

"And if we don't?" Snarly grinds out.

Alaric smiles, his mouth transforming for just a moment to show his shifted canines, before changing them back. "By all means, stay. I can't promise it will end well for you though."

Yes, wolfman. Let's get them together.

The shorter vamp with dark brown hair looks at both of us, then his friends, and gives a slight bow of his head before walking straight to the door.

"Coward!" Snarly yells after him.

"Smart, I'd say," Alaric murmurs. "And what about you? We really only need to speak with your buddy here."

Snarly looks back to Evan, who shakes his head slightly. I wonder if he means "no, don't fight" or "no, don't leave." But Snarly grabs his beer and stalks past us as he leaves the room.

My eyes are trained on Evan while he watches Alaric.

"Oomph!" I jolt forward, straight into a chair, a massive pain in my back.

Without so much as a warning, Alaric shifts in front of me. His clothes and weapons disappear into the ether, and then he's standing in front of me, more than half my height, covered with his deep gray fur. He dives straight for Snarly, teeth bared. A hiss of pain follows as his maw goes right through the vamp's arm. Alaric rips his head to the side and tears the vamp's arm off.

I stare, dumbfounded, until I hear a noise behind me and realize Evan is about to split. I turn and chase him down a long thin hall. Anticipation and anxiety tear at my insides, leaving a twisted feeling in my chest. He reaches the end of the hall and three doors, then turns to the right. I pull some spray out of my pocket and follow him.

"Stop!" I shout. "You're only going to make this worse!"

I race into a large sitting room and come to a halt. He's got a long sword in his right hand, standing in a ready position but somewhat distracted by the shattering of glass from the other room.

"Just turn yourself over. This is a mistake."

He snarls and flashes forward. His sword swishes towards me in an arc. I manage to jump to the side to avoid his blade. He pursues me. It's a dance—a deadly dance. He takes a step forward. Me back. His blade nicks my arm, and I hiss at the hot slice over my forearm.

A loud crack sounds from the other room, and then a meaty thud. Feet pound towards us. I step back so I have a view of the door as nausea rolls through my stomach at the thought of who the victim of the broken bone was.

Alaric steps through the door and my shoulders drop in relief. I suck in air as another hot slice of the sword goes through my forearm..

Son of a—

"You stupid bitch," Evan yells. "Just get out of the way! Stop searching!"

"Searching for who?" Alaric calls, attracting his attention.

Before he can answer, I lift the silver spray, step to the side, and unleash it into Evan's eyes. He immediately claws his face, hissing and snarling. I've never used silver spray before, but the damage it causes is enough that I almost lose my lunch. Evan's eyes are burning away, pieces of them missing, and the smell of singed flesh doesn't help either.

Alaric walks up to me and smiles, a proud look aimed my way. "Well done." He turns to Evan and pulls some lined, silver cuffs from his belt. He grabs one of Evan's hands, locks it into place, then rips the other one behind him as he snaps the cuffs in place.

I look away from Evan's eyes, knowing he won't be able to start healing until the silver is removed.

Fuck him. Bastard deserves it.

"Let's go. I need to take him back to headquarters. You can drive. I'll sit in the back with our new friend here."

"You don't need to read him his rights or something like that?"

His answering smile looks dangerous with blood staining his teeth. "No need in this case. Orpheus and the Council have declared this a domestic terror case because of the numbers."

Evan stills despite the wincing on his face and labored breathing, but he says nothing.

"Lead the way, then."

Alaric pulls Evan around, and shoves him roughly towards his front door, holding him by the left arm. Evan makes little resistance trussed up in the cuffs, and instead goes where he's directed.

When we make it onto the street, my phone vibrates in my pocket. An uneasy feeling passes through me, and I pull it out to look.

Unknown: Be careful you aren't so busy catching pawns that you lose your own important pieces. Consider yourself warned.

APPEARANCES

ALARIC DIRECTS ME THROUGH a back entrance to the Council building that I didn't know existed. I follow the driveway until we get to a set of giant metal doors.

"Just pull up here," Alaric says.

As soon as the car rolls to a stop, he gets out with Evan, shoving him roughly in the direction of the doors. Alaric pauses and looks back at me.

"You might be better off heading home rather than coming in. This isn't always the nicest part of the job, especially in cases like this."

My insides are at war, my heart full of warmth but my stomach a twist of nerves.

Why should Alaric have to do it alone when we can share the emotional load?

"It's all right," I murmur, putting the car into park and getting out after them. "I signed up for this. Let's go."

Alaric locks gazes with mine a moment longer, then nods. "Follow me."

I walk behind them, somewhat surprised that Evan hasn't said anything in a while. Alaric leads us down one hallway, then another, and into what is clearly an interrogation room. Both a metal chair and table are in the center of the room, and along the walls are shelves of implements sectioned into groups according to what would hurt different supernatural species.

Gee, I certainly haven't seen this side of things before.

I stand to the side and watch as Alaric puts Evan into the chair and straps him down, hands flat on the ends of the wide chair arms. Alaric then douses Evan's face in water, using a bucket placed on the ground beside his chair. The straps mustn't be silver because Evan's face starts healing and he hisses in pain. Healing at that speed doesn't look enjoyable.

I guess we're playing nice cop first. Sort of?

As soon as Evan is healed, Alaric begins. "So. Evan. Why were you trying to break into Everleigh's apartment?"

"Because I was told to," he says deadpan.

"By whom?" Alaric rumbles, clearly annoyed by the vague answer.

Evan grins, his lips pulling so tightly, they match the color of the rest of his skin. "By my boss."

Alaric snarls. "I'm going to give you one more chance to do this the easy way."

"Okay. Okay." Evan pulls an exaggerated thinking face. "Definitely... your momma."

I barely manage to contain a snort, and then watch with a tight stomach as Alaric goes to the collection of implements that are clearly meant for vampires. He picks up a wooden stake and I stand taller, hesitant about his choice. Killing Evan straight away won't help us.

With no warning, Alaric walks back to Evan and slams the stake through his left hand. Evan lets out an inhuman screech that has me covering my ears.

There's the Parisian wolf.

"So. Your boss's name?"

Evan heaves breaths in and out. "Fuck you," he spits.

Alaric shrugs, reaches into his back pocket to retrieve another stake that I completely missed, and stabs it straight through Evan's other hand. Evan's scream is raspier this time, but no less high pitched.

"You fucking asshole!"

"Your boss's name?" Alaric says simply.

I feel the demonic side of me stir, and heat builds in me as I watch Alaric command the situation with no emotion. Brutal. Efficient.

Hot.

Evan watches him through furious eyes, then turns to look at me, and a dangerous glint flickers. "You worried the boss wants to fuck your girlfriend over there? Or maybe you want to let me out so I can do it." He leers at me, and I barely see Alaric move before another stake goes right through Evan's crotch.

Alaric suddenly looks a lot less calm and a whole lot more murderous. He snarls this time when Evan screams, then passes out for a moment. I stay quiet, arousal coiling in my core at Alaric's strength and protectiveness.

Alaric's eyes flash to mine. They're full of anger and heat. *Possession?*

I can possess him.

He spins and throws another bucket of water over Evan, causing him to come to.

"Ready to share yet, Evan? Or, if you'd prefer, I can start removing body parts instead?" His words are a growl, his neutrality gone.

Evan tries to speak but can't. Alaric twists one of the stakes in Evan's hands. He tries to speak again, only managing a whisper. Alaric leans in close to hear him, then stands and pats him on the head.

"Not quite a name, but it'll do for now. That wasn't so hard, was it?" He looks over to me. "Let's go."

I glance at Evan and the stakes still in him, the angelic side of me unable to leave things as they are when we have what we need. I pull my brows up and look between Alaric and Evan, clearly showing what I want.

A rumble comes from Alaric's chest and ricochets through my insides.

"I'll send someone in to take out the stakes and lock him up until we need him again."

Satisfied, I follow Alaric out.

An hour later, we're sitting in Orpheus's office in the Council building waiting for him to arrive. Alaric is in a new pair of tight, dark jeans and a charcoal gray shirt, and I realize I'm still wearing his jacket.

I stand up to take it off, but his stormy eyes catch mine. "Keep it for tonight. I've got more."

I shuck it back on, not upset in the slightest at keeping his alluring scent so close. "Sure."

Orpheus marches into the office and takes a seat at his desk, his dark skin absorbing the light of the fire behind him. "I hear you have a prisoner and some information?"

"Yes. The prisoner gave us the location where we might find his boss. Unfortunately, according to the records, many of the council vampires live in that area of the city. Also, according to the records we have, his coven leader is Louisa, but Everleigh's latest vision clearly shows a male vampire. I was wondering if we might arrange another meeting and use him as bait to draw out whoever he is loyal to?"

Orpheus puts an elbow on his desk and leans forward to rest his chin on his hand, pondering Alaric's request. He sucks his lips between his teeth, then sits back and looks at us both.

"Very well. I shall organize a... get-together... with the male vampire members from the council. Two nights from now at my estate. Ensure you come formally attired and bring the prisoner. You should all arrive before the guests—say 10:00 p.m. I'm sure that will be long enough to make everyone sweat."

He pushes his chair back from his desk and stands. "I have something else to attend to. You are both dismissed."

I can almost feel Alaric bristle beside me, but Orpheus's behavior and being ignored completely by supes isn't new to me. I offer a haphazard bow and turn to leave, glancing sideways at Alaric as I do. He stands abruptly, causing his chair to scuff on the floor, and follows me out.

"I'll drive you home," he says in the hallway, his tone still brisk. "Let's go."

Since I'm still vision-free, the vamp who tried to get into my apartment is locked up, and Raine has been stuck inside for too long, I decide we deserve a night out.

I stick my head around Raine's doorway. "Hey, get some dressy clothes on. I'm going to take you out to the supe bar just outside the city. You can get a better taste of our life, so to speak, in the flesh. Plus, I can introduce you to Clara."

Her face lights up, "Oh, your sister! I can't wait to meet her. How long until we're planning to leave?"

I look at my smartphone. "Let's say about an hour. No sense in showing up too early, and that gives us plenty of time to get ready."

An hour later, we're both at the door. Raine looks sexy as all hells in a Victorian-style corset, black jeans, and her reddish-brown hair done in drop curls. I whistle in appreciation, and she laughs.

"You look pretty great yourself! I adore the shade of green in your dress. And those black stilettos look like they could kill."

I grin back at her. "They might just be able to do that. Come on. Let's go and have some fun." I flick my straightened hair behind one shoulder and grab my clutch. "There's a taxi waiting for us downstairs."

When we arrive near the venue and I lead her down an abandoned street, Raine looks at me in question.

"Don't worry. It's here. There's protection on this street to keep unwanted visitors away."

I lead her to the door and gesture for her to open it with her new vamp muscles. She easily yanks it open but realizes it's way heavier than a normal door. I walk in first, just so I can watch Raine's expression as she sees the décor and the half-dressed, ruggedly handsome guards.

Her mouth pops open into a little *O* shape as she takes in all the details. She wanders from one side to the other, looking at everything with a fierce sense of curiosity. I peek over at the bodyguards, who ignore my existence after my last visit, and snort at their poor attempts to keep straight faces while watching Raine. Especially when she bends over to see the lowest shelves. Her curves in those clothes are killer.

"Come on, Raine. Let's get a table."

As soon as I utter those words, the wolves straighten their postures and their expressions.

I lead Raine past them and to the tables by the bar. I wave at Clara, who follows me and Raine with her gaze until she sees us take a seat, nods to me in acknowledgment, and returns to her work.

I spend the next couple of hours drinking with Raine and pointing out the different types of supes in the room until she begins to make a game of guessing them herself.

Clara saunters over, a black towel from the bar tucked into her back pocket. She leans forward and kisses me on each cheek. "Sister, who have you brought in today?"

"This is Raine. She's a newly turned vampire. I'm just showing her the ropes."

She pulls her gaze from Raine back to me, a frown marring her flawless face. "Why are you doing that? She's the vamps' fucking responsibility."

Heat rushes to my chest at her poor behavior. "I got a vision. She needs help, and I'm helping," I say stiffly.

"You're ridiculous, Everleigh. This is not your job. Just ignore the visions as I do. We owe no fealty. We are not required to support the cause."

I sit perfectly still in my seat as knots twist in my stomach, and I realize I've not mentioned another important thing to someone. I also know giving myself away right now is worse than a bad idea. Clara won't like it and a public tantrum is really too much attention for me.

She sighs, gives Raine a once-over, and then looks back to me. "I'm not interested in your stray unless she wants to help the... cause. Don't bother bringing her to see me again."

"Hey!" Raine says. "That's enough. I'm not some *thing* and your sister doesn't deserve to be treated like that. Don't be such a cow."

Clara has murder in her eyes, but she turns and stalks back to the bar without a word. I peek at Raine, guilt and shame for my sister's behavior riding me, but so much gratitude for her having my back filling my heart. To my surprise, she puts a hand on my arm and gives it a little squeeze, sympathy in her soft brown eyes.

"Why don't we go get some ice cream and head back to your place?" she offers.

"Yeah. Awesome. Ice cream sounds perfect about now."

We walk back out the main doors, and I keep my eyes trained on the door to avoid Clara. Back on the street, I say to Raine, "I'm so sorry about her. She's usually pretty standoffish but I didn't think she'd be straight-up rude. Maybe things aren't going well with her at the moment."

Raine stops, grabbing my arm to pull me to a halt. "Hey. It's not your fault, okay? She gets to make her own choices. Are you all right?"

I shake my head slightly. "How can you be so sweet about everything, especially after your own life got turned upside down? Clara's had a lot more years to pull it together than you have."

She shrugs, her curls springing around like coils. "We just see things differently, I guess. What did she mean about helping?"

I roll my eyes, feeling a dull ache in my head when they reach the top. "I'm actually a bit shocked she mentioned it. She spends her time hunting demons when she's not at the bar listening for those she thinks need to be punished."

Confusion appears on Raine's face. "Um. Aren't you both part demon?"

I sigh. "Yes. But—" I swallow the lump in my throat. "—our mother and father were killed by a demon, so Clara tries to put down any who aren't sticking to the laws."

"So, she's like an enforcer for demons or something?"

I laugh so hard that I cough. "Don't ever let her hear you say that. She hates enforcers. She does her own thing. It's lucky she hasn't been caught, really."

Raine nods, expression serious. "I won't say anything. I promise."

I pull Raine in for a quick hug, surprise filling me at how quickly I've become fond of her. "Let's go get that ice cream."

On Monday night, Alaric stands at my apartment door wearing an ink-black suit with a grayish-silver tie. He looks good enough to eat.

Yes, please!

"You look beautiful," he says huskily with a slight tinge of pink on his cheeks.

As much as I don't like Orpheus, his demand that we dress in formal wear for the party feels way less stupid and far more worth it right now.

"Thank you," I murmur, warmth rising to my face. "You look rather handsome yourself."

The moment holds for a few seconds until Raine bursts into the room with my clutch. She skids to a halt with an embarrassed look on her face.

"Sorry! I didn't mean to, uh, interrupt. You almost left without this. I added the stuff you asked me for earlier. I hope you two have fun." She flushes a shade darker than I've ever seen another vampire manage and adds, "Oh, uh, sorry again. Hope you catch the guy."

She pulls me in for a hug, which I readily return, before adding, "Be safe."

Alaric and I head down to the car together, side by side despite the tight staircase, and an excited tingle rushes through me at Alaric's closeness. We don't say anything as we walk down, but it feels nice in a way I've never allowed myself to experience before due to my self-imposed supernatural exile.

Alaric opens my door, and I get in without a word. I'm not sure what to say. A short pause later, he clears his throat and leaves me to close the door on my own.

After a few moments of quiet, he says, "Orpheus sent something for Evan to wear so he'll be dressed appropriately for the party by the time we arrive to collect him. Are you all clear on the plan?"

"Yes. I've got it. I have the few weapons you suggested in my bag, though I don't see Orpheus letting me use them. Do you?"

He shakes his head from side to side. "Unlikely, but they're insurance in case anything happens. If it's going to be us or them, it's us. This could easily turn to shit tonight."

"Do you think it will? That anonymous text message suggested to me that our vamp is in this for the long game. He won't out himself in such an obvious way."

"Probably not, but hopefully we'll at least find the next piece of the puzzle. I feel we're getting closer to solving this."

We collect Evan and the rest of the trip is silent. Once we arrive at our destination, a vampire valet takes Alaric's keys and moves the car to a parking area down the lane. Different from last time, but since Alaric just handed the keys off, I suppose he was expecting it.

Inside, Orpheus comes out in a suit the color of venous blood. I'm not sure if it's a fashion statement or a threat, and I decide it's best not to comment.

"Ah, Evan. Our guest for the evening. Come."

Unsurprisingly, Evan has nothing smart to say to his king, even if he won't share the name of his boss with him. While Orpheus rules all vampires, it's their coven leaders and political alliances that most affect their day-to-day life.

We follow Orpheus to the end of the hallway, except this time, we turn to the left and enter a large room set up for a party. A buffet is filled with blood displayed in various containers and a few typical human foods vampires might consume after their stomach is lined with blood. I've watched a vampire eat human food on an empty stomach. It's like watching food poisoning on steroids. I suppose the food might also be for Alaric and me, but I certainly won't be eating it—you don't consume the food of supes you don't trust.

Orpheus walks straight to a throne-like chair that has been placed on a small dais at the end of the room. I expect him to take a seat, but he turns to Evan and points to the chair. "Sit. Now."

Evan's swallow is audible, and a little piece of me feels bad. Being the bait is never fun. Especially when it is so obvious. But either way, he lowers himself in silence.

"Good," the king says dismissively, then turns to focus his attention on us. "Now—you pair. I suggest making yourselves comfortable in the seats near the wall. The best vantage point between the doors and the bait."

When Alaric doesn't respond, I jump in. "Right. Sitting." I walk off towards the wall and heave a sigh of relief when I hear footsteps following me. One drama is enough for tonight.

Vampires enter and talk among themselves, some drinking while others eat. Almost everyone looks at Evan and us—only once—then ignores us all. After Evan's been shown off for long enough, Orpheus summons the fifteen or so vampires to the throne as well as us.

"Welcome, one and all. I do know we haven't had one of these gatherings in some time, and I thought it was high time to rectify the matter. And as always, I come bearing entertainment." He looks around the circle, catching each vampire's eyes, one at a time.

The tension in the room ratchets up, everyone clearly unsure what is about to happen.

"A question first, friends. Who is it that Evan belongs to?"

A few seconds tick by and the intensity in the room sucks me in. My limbs lock into place as I attempt to look around without making direct eye contact.

"Come now. Surely someone here must know?" Orpheus prompts.

One of the council members, Horus, answers in a bored monotone, "I believe he is one of Louisa's lot."

Orpheus breaks into a feral grin. "Right you are, Horus. Right you are. *But* it seems Evan here is loyal to someone else as well. Someone in this room."

The vampires who were breathing as a matter of habit stop. And now the only breaths are mine and Alaric's. The vamps are all still. Prey trying to avoid the predator.

"Evan." He shifts his gaze to the vamp in the chair. "Would you like to tell us who it is?"

Blood pools in Evan's eyes but he shakes his head. Outing the vampire would result in a fate worse than death.

Orpheus pouts theatrically. "Hmm. A shame." He turns to the rest of the vampires and looks at each of them in turn.

The intensity in the room has my heart racing loud enough for the vamps to hear it. Luckily for me, they have bigger concerns.

Orpheus begins walking. He moves to the first vampire and asks, "Is he yours?"

After six vampires have been asked and denied he is theirs, Elias, the angry vampire from the council meeting, steps forward. "He's mine, for fuck's sake! What the deepest realm of hells is this about? We all have vampires on our payroll from other covens, just like you do."

The vampire king turns in slow motion, a maniacal smile on his face. Elias is the vamp who's been causing him a lot of problems. The victory couldn't be any sweeter for him.

He glances at Evan. "Are you loyal to Elias?"

Since he can't get into trouble now, Evan nods and slumps back into the throne. Horror and defeat ripple across his face, and I can't help but be curious about the reaction.

"Well, in that case." Orpheus clicks, and all eyes dart toward him, then to the doorway, where two women walk in with what appears to be a black blanket in their hands.

Before anyone can move, Orpheus streaks forward and slams a wooden stake into the center of Elias's chest, and he immediately drops to the floor with a thud. Several of the vampires around the room hiss and jump back, fear riding their once carefully neutral faces.

The thuds in my chest are louder and faster. It's only when the women cast the black blanket over Elias on the floor that I hear, and then smell, the sound of sizzling flesh. Nausea bubbles in my stomach and moves up my esophagus with a burning sensation.

Orpheus clicks and the women pull the blanket away, leaving behind a thin, almost delicate-looking silver chain net. Elias glares at Orpheus with the fury of a thousand burning suns, but he can't speak.

Can't move.

When I look up, I see the other vampires have scattered, deserting their drinks and food.

"Well, there you have it." Orpheus announces, brushing some imaginary lint off his immaculate coat. "I've solved the case. Go lock him up."

HUNTED

"It was too easy," I say to Raine for probably the fifteenth time since I got home last night. "Alaric thought so too. Why would Elias just come forward like that?!"

I stuff a mouthful of imported Count Chocula cereal into my mouth and crunch it while my new friend looks on in sympathy. After she was turned, she saw the cereal online and laughed so much that I had to get it for her. Now we eat it every day.

"If he wasn't the one—and I think you're right about that—I'm sure something will give it away. More new vampires or something. He won't get away with it."

I huff out a sharp breath. "You're right. I know you are. But someone innocent is probably getting tortured right now for an answer they don't have. And why did Alaric insist on doing the interrogation on his own this time? We were meant to be doing this together. Ridiculous."

Raine puts her cereal on the small table and comes and wraps her arm around me, giving me a gentle squeeze. "It'll be okay, Ev. Just give it a little time. You can't do anything about what's happening at the Council. Oh, speaking of, have you heard from Raphael?"

"Hmm. No. Now that you mention it, he hasn't called." I look at my smartphone on the little table and wonder if he'll make another impeccably timed call, but when nothing happens, I go back to my cereal.

I lie on the small balcony in the midday sun in my bikini, focusing on the feeling of hot air traveling down through my mouth and into my lungs, expanding them with an almost burn, before letting the air out again. I flick to the next page of the romance novel I borrowed from Raine before a feeling of dread pools in my stomach. Once my sight fades to white, I can see a different place.

An almost full moon. A cemetery. Mausoleums.

A grave. The ground tremors. The dirt moves.

A hand shoots up through the disturbed earth.

"Dammit!" I exclaim, and Raine is almost immediately at the balcony door, concern in every line of her face.

"What is it? A vision?"

I nod and point for her to go back inside. I follow and then shut the door to make sure we have privacy. "Yes. Another vampire being turned."

She pauses for a beat. "Could it be someone else responsible?"

I shake my head. "I don't think so. They're coming out of the same grave as yours."

Her brows inch down in the center. "Do you ever re-see old visions or something? Could you just be remembering me maybe?"

"Not often, but also, the hand that came out of the grave belonged to a man."

She nods with a serious look. "Who do you need to contact? Do you think Orpheus will believe you? I know you said he was hells-bent on it being that Elias guy, the one he hates."

"Honestly, I don't even know if he'll take a call from me now that he has someone to blame. I mean, it'll come out eventually when more bodies show up, but if we can stop that from happening, that would be better. Alaric and the enforcers already rounded up the rest of the newly turned vamps, so it's not like it won't be noticed."

"So, you'll call Alaric then?"

"Yeah. I'll let him know, especially since this means it can't be Elias."

Raine and I meet Henry down the street for dinner since the moon isn't full enough tonight to match my vision of the newest vampire rising. Still, Alaric assured me he would have someone watching, just in case.

We perch at a round high-top table and wait for our burgers to arrive.

"So, what did you teach before all of this happened?" Henry asks Raine, watching her intently.

She tucks her hair behind her ear. "Oh, primary school mostly. The younger kids. I've always loved working with little ones." She leans forward and Henry joins her. "The teenagers scare me a little if I'm honest!"

He sits back and chuckles warmly. "I can understand that. My nephew, John, is trouble. Great kid, but I mean... trapped in a classroom trying to teach him something he doesn't wanna hear? No thanks."

As they move back and forth about their jobs, my phone vibrates.

Alaric: Can you come and see if proximity to Elias will give you more info about the case? We need to find some more solid evidence. Orpheus won't accept the vision as enough proof to set him free.

Gee. No pressure. Find a more concrete clue or, my guess, Orpheus is going to kill Elias out of some ridiculous combination of hatred and political power.

Me: Yeah. I can try. I need to get Raine and Henry home, then I can come in. Hold tight.

Alaric: I'll come get you.

Me: Okay, sure.

When I look up, I see Henry and Raine staring at me.

"Sorry, guys! I didn't mean to stop paying attention, but I need to help Alaric with something, so I have to get Raine home. Would it be okay if we take the burgers to go?"

Raine's face falls a little, but she tries to put on a smile. "Sure. That's okay."

Henry looks at her, then over to me. "How about we finish dinner here, and then we can share a taxi home? I'm sure we'll be fine at this busy restaurant."

I look at Raine, and my heart feels like it's being pierced. I scan the packed restaurant and pull my lips to one side, thinking.

"All right. It is busy here. Just don't stay too late and go home in a taxi. Don't walk. And go together. Agreed?"

"Agreed," they chorus, grinning like little kids who just got their way.

I shake my head in amusement and try to ignore the niggle in my stomach that something is going to go wrong. It doesn't feel like one of my "from above" kind of messages, just worry over friends I've never really had before.

Me: Change of plans. They're getting a taxi. I can head in now.

Alaric: Send me the address. I'm already on my way.

Yes, sir.

I flick him a message with the restaurant's address and wait for him to arrive, trying to stay present with Henry and Raine even though my mind is determined to wander to where I'm going with Alaric.

Once Alaric arrives, I stand and give Henry and Raine a squeeze goodbye.

"Bye, Ev!" they call, and then laugh before continuing to chat.

I wave and head off to Alaric's car.

I follow Alaric into the same room where Evan was interrogated, unable to keep my eyes off his fine rear-end as he walks, each step showing his muscles—he clearly works out.

Inside the room, Elias is sprawled out on the metal table, but I can tell immediately from the smell of burned flesh that his restraints are made of silver. When I get close enough, my steps falter. Elias looks at us through a small, square-shaped silver net that rests on his face. One eye is partially gone from the fine chains, the other holds death.

Alaric stops when he hears my movements lose consistency and turns to me. "Orpheus," he says in explanation.

I pause, thinking through my next question. "Could we take the silver off?" I point to his face, which is shredded, bleeding, and blistered from the consistent damage. Moving his mouth would open every wound further. "We can't talk to him like this."

After looking at the door, Alaric bobs his head in agreement, and walks over to the prisoner. He picks up a pair of gloves and puts them on, then pauses for a second, and mutters something to himself. Alaric removes all the cuffs first, adds straps as replacements, and then he peels off the small net. Despite trying to do it all quickly, Alaric's movements tear Elias's skin as it separates from the silver. Once all the silver has been removed, Elias begins to heal. He hisses and groans in pain.

Standing quietly, I wait until his face and eyes are whole again, then I approach.

The death promised in his single eye is gone and replaced with relief. He waits until I meet his black eyes. "I'm not used to saying it, but thank you. I told that fucking bastard it wasn't me who was turning people. He holds too much of a grudge to give a shit. Just kept finding ways to torture me. Can you get me out of here?"

Alaric steps forward again on his other side and talks before I have a chance. His tone is hard and unforgiving. "We can't just let you out when you've been accused. You know that. What can you tell us about Evan?"

Elias rolls his head to look at Alaric and manages to keep his tone neutral. "I've already told that prick everything I know. Evan's only job for me was to feed me information about Louisa's clan and occasionally provide false information. My agenda is to dethrone Orpheus and take his place." Elias shrugs. "I'm his competition. I wouldn't do something this stupid."

Inclined to agree with his reasoning, I glance at Alaric to gauge his reaction. He doesn't show much on his face in response to Elias's words, and instead looks at me. "Can you see if touching him gives you a vision?"

Elias snorts at Alaric's suggestion and says to me, "Go ahead."

I technically don't need permission, but I feel better having it since I don't believe Elias is guilty in this case. Though I'm sure that being hundreds of years old and vying for the vampire throne, he's got skeletons in his closet I'd rather not know about.

I reach out and touch his arm, close my eyes, and concentrate on opening my mind to a vision. I don't usually need to, but since I'm trying to initiate one, it could help. After a minute, I take my hand away.

"Nothing," I say, frowning. "I don't think we're on the right path here."

Alaric dips his head in acknowledgment but says nothing. I suppose working for the Council means not saying stuff like that in front of the prisoners, and I grimace.

"Right!" Elias bursts out. "Tell *his Highness* that, would you? I don't intend to rot down here, and he better watch his back after this."

I huff out a breath and chuckle. "I'm not a vamp or anything, but I'm going to suggest that kind of threat won't get you out of here any sooner."

He shrugs. "I'm willing to bet the bastard won't let me out of here until you've found whoever is really responsible."

I frown, irritated at the unjust behavior, and my chest tightens knowing I can't do anything about it. "Sadly, I won't be taking that bet. I think you're right. We're doing our best."

He tilts his head at me, and his face is serious. "You're not so bad, you know, for a hybrid."

I snort and shake my head. "Come on, Alaric. Let's go."

I walk over and open the door, heading straight out, hearing Alaric following behind. As I round the corner, I jerk to a halt, nearly crashing straight into Raphael.

"Jesus!"

One side of his mouth jerks up. "Not quite."

His eyes bring out the golden glow of my own, and my breath quickens when his light up in return. I see him concentrate for a moment, then his glow fades out, and I feel my own withdraw. He chooses not to say anything about it, so I don't bother him with more questions he likely doesn't know the answer to yet.

"What are you doing down here?"

"I could ask you the same, though I am already aware. Having removed all that silver will not please Orpheus when he returns later this evening."

I shrug. "Elias didn't do it. Orpheus knows that. He just refuses to listen. Another vampire is about to be turned and will likely rise tomorrow evening. It can hardly be Elias doing the turning when he's locked up. I don't suppose you'd like to convince Orpheus of that?"

Raphael tilts his head, a hint of curiosity and something else in his eyes. "No angels generally talk to me in such a way. You are... unique. In more ways than the obvious, it seems."

I sigh, uncomfortable with his assessment, but wanting this problem solved. "So, that's a *no* then?"

He shakes his head. "I cannot interfere directly in the interrogation of Orpheus's own vampire. Especially not without consulting the Council. I'm afraid Elias will be staying put. At least if he stays until another is turned, the evidence will be solid enough that Orpheus must release him."

"Yes, though the tradeoff for that is going to be more human lives. One turned and potentially more attacked. Hopefully, we have enough in place to stop that happening."

He stills. "You think human lives are worth as much as the vampire's? As ours?"

"I see no reason to believe they are worth less just because they are different to us."

"Hmm," he murmurs. "An unusual view to have."

"I suppose when you grow up being treated as 'less than', it is easier to empathize."

"Perhaps," he says quietly.

Raphael cocks his head as though he is being called, then says, "I am needed. I shall try to keep Orpheus occupied while you both continue to solve this case. That ought to give Elias a little longer away from the silver."

I bow to Raphael in thanks and acknowledgment, but when I rise, he's already gone. Alaric walks up beside me.

"Well, that was an interesting conversation," he says.

"It was," I agree. "Where to next?"

I knock on my apartment door and wait for Raine to answer. After almost thirty seconds of silence, I rummage through my bag, my stomach in knots. I jam the key into the door and yank it open.

"Raine?" I call loudly.

Nothing.

I rush around the apartment, looking everywhere to be sure. Everything is the same as when we left earlier.

Maybe they're just still out?

I hit dial. Her phone rings out.

Shit.

I call Henry's number. It goes straight to voicemail.

"Shit. Shit. Shit."

I ring Alaric and he picks up after only a few seconds. "Is everything okay?"

"No!" I half yell into the phone. "Something is wrong. Raine isn't here, and neither she nor Henry are answering their phones. They wouldn't do that with everything happening right now."

"Right. I'm turning around. I'll make some calls. Meet me out front."

He hangs up without another word, and I relock the door and slam it shut. I rush down the stairs, heart racing, and then pace back and forth on the sidewalk, waiting for Alaric to get back.

Why is this happening? Why didn't I get a vision or some intuition about this? I never should have left them at dinner. This is all my fault.

Whoever is responsible is going to pay for this.

Alaric pulls up on the other side of the road, his brakes screeching as his car rolls to a stop. I run over and yank the door open.

"Anything?" I ask desperately.

"No. Nothing yet. Let's go back to the restaurant and check there." He pauses as he turns the car around, then adds, "They wouldn't have gone back to Henry's together, would they? And didn't mention it because they knew you were busy."

My feet bounce up and down as I try to contain my anxiety. "I don't think so. They promised they'd take cabs back to their own places. I don't think either of them would risk it with Raine still being so new, even if she has great self-control."

"We'll find them, okay? I've got the tech team tracking down their smartphones. They'll call back any—"

His cell rings and he answers it immediately. Someone talks to him on the other end, and his frown pulls the knots in my stomach tighter. "Right. Check the surrounding cameras in that area and get back to me."

He hangs up, and then reaches out and begins rubbing soft circles on the top of my hand, trying to comfort me. His gesture both warms my heart and has dread pooling in my stomach because I know whatever he is about to say isn't good.

"They found the phones. Henry's is dead, but they tracked his last known location to the restaurant. Raine's is in the same place. They checked the restaurant cameras as well. They've been gone for a couple of hours."

I tip my head back against the seat and focus on the feel of Alaric's warm skin, and breathing. *In. Out. In. Out. In. Out.* My heart burns as though cut with a knife.

How could I be so irresponsible?

Alaric brings the car to a halt. He pulls his hand away and it feels like the last piece of warmth I had drains away.

"Come on, Everleigh. Losing it is not going to help. We still have time. Help me search the area."

I squeeze my eyes shut, suck in a breath, and blow it out through my nose.

Right. We can do this. Finding Henry and Raine. That's what matters.

I open the door and jump out. "I'll check this side of the block," I say, pointing to my left, "and you check the other side."

"Got it."

Alaric rushes off and I make my way to my own side. I look inside the restaurant, and in the parking lot. I check the bathrooms, and then pause at the mouth of a dark alleyway. Dread threatens to drown me when I see the glint of smashed glass next to a dumpster. I move closer.

It's a smashed phone. I reach down hesitantly and move some chunks to check out the back. My heart sinks. It's Henry's. His small cowboy hat sticker is holding together a few broken pieces of his case. Tears roll down my cheeks and, with little hope, I try again to call Raine's number.

Her upbeat ringtone sounds from the dumpster beside me, and my knees hit the asphalt with a thud. I close my eyes, no longer able to stop the cascade of tears.

Footsteps rush toward me, and I can't even bring myself to look.

I feel the warmth of a body close to me, then smell Alaric's woodsy scent. "I'm sorry, Everleigh. They couldn't find anything on the cameras in the area, but some have been destroyed. They called with a more precise location of the phones, so I came straight here."

I stare at the ground, hearing Alaric's words, but no response comes. No vision comes. There's nothing. No hope. My friends are going to be killed—if they aren't already dead.

"This is all my fault, Alaric. If I'd just stayed with them, or better, stayed away entirely... didn't try to make friends, they wouldn't be gone right now." I shake my head. "You should stay away too. I'm like poison. No one is safe near me." My voice cracks along with another fracture in my heart. "No one."

RELENTLESS

ALARIC KNEELS IN FRONT of me, and his warm fingers gently touch my chin to lift my gaze to his.

"This isn't your fault, Everleigh. You aren't responsible for what other supes choose to do. That's on them. I know all you want to do right now is crumble, but this is the most crucial time." He moves his hand down and takes mine. "We need to get up from this alley. We need to do a wider search. We need to find a clue. There's always a clue."

Alaric hesitates for a moment. "Can you help me with this? If you can't, it's okay. I can take you home, but I don't think you'd forgive yourself if you left now."

I stare at him, struggling to process his words. Needing them to sink in. Because on the surface, the words sound right. I wouldn't be able to live with myself if I never even tried. I close my eyes and try to pull myself together enough to do this. To be there for my friends, even if I fear the worst.

Alaric's presence is reassuring. He isn't talking. He's not forcing me to choose, or even rushing me despite the need to get moving. The little bit of comfort he gives me is enough to help me move. To not feel alone in this for now. I open my eyes and take a deep breath.

"You're right. I need to do this. What do we do?"

He nods with respect in his eyes, and then stands and helps me to my feet.

"First, let's go into the Council building and see the tech team. I've asked them to collect footage from the last few days to see if we can find anyone that has been following you and Raine or Henry."

A touch of hope sparks in my chest. "Right. Okay. Good idea."

We walk through the Council lobby to the lifts. When we get inside, Alaric pushes the button for the thirteenth floor.

"We will find them, okay?" he says. "And they will be all right."

Despair floods my chest and pushes up to my throat, causing me to remain speechless. I try to smile, but I'm sure it doesn't look right.

When the ding sounds, I follow Alaric out and down a sparse hall, and then through a door that says, Office of Enforcement. There's a reception desk inside the door, but the lady behind it merely glances up, sees Alaric, and returns to whatever she is doing. She doesn't even bother to ask who I am or what I'm doing here. And honestly, I'm glad.

Down the hall, there's a heavy-looking door with Technical Division written on it and a pin pad on the side. Alaric types in a code and pushes the door forward. He holds it open for me, and I trail in behind him. Despite my frayed emotions, I still gaze in awe at the setup. There are computers and screens everywhere, and about a dozen employees scattered around the room.

"Alaric," a female with long, red hair calls out. "Over here."

Alaric gestures to the woman sitting in front of three screens. "Everleigh, this is Tessa. She's in charge of the tech department. Tessa, this is Everleigh."

Tessa gives me a cursory look up and down, then holds out a hand for me to shake. "Sorry to be meeting you under these circumstances."

"Thank you," I murmur, unsure what else to say but feeling an intense urge to shout at her to tell me she has found something.

"Any updates?" Alaric asks, filling in the brief silence.

Tessa shakes her head. "I've got the twins over there"—she jerks her head towards the back corner of the room where one male and one female watch four screens each—"looking at local surveillance videos around the areas you mentioned."

When I concentrate a little harder, it seems the videos are running at double speed. "How are they—"

"The twins, Oldin and Stella, are vamps. They always watch like this. Don't worry, Everleigh. I promise they're thorough. They won't miss a thing."

Chastised, I nod. There's no reason to be picky about how they work. They clearly know what they're doing. Refocusing my attention between Alaric and Tessa, I ask, "What can I do to help?"

Tessa bobs her head up and down, thankfully ignoring my rude behavior. "We have one blind spot so far. I assume you went to the supe club outside the city in the last few days? Stella flagged you and Raine going into the area but the wards there prevented any kind of camera detection from working." She frowns. "There are a lot of ways out of that place that we can't follow. Is there anyone inside who might know if you were followed out?"

A little relief pierces my raincloud of emotions. "Yes. I can call my sister. She works there."

Alaric waves me toward a little booth but stays with Tessa.

Inside, I call the club, knowing Clara never answers her phone. If I have a chance of getting her, it will be there. After what feels like an eternity, she answers the call directly. "Yes?"

I shake my head. "Clara? It's Everleigh."

Silence for a moment. The noises coming through the phone indicate Clara is moving. "What do you need?"

I grimace at her remark, but since she isn't wrong this time, I suck it up. "Just a quick question. The night I was there with Raine, my new friend, do you remember it?"

"Your new pet project," she says snarkily. "The one who called me a cow. I remember."

My teeth grind together, my jaw straining before I force it to relax. "I'm aware you don't particularly care for her, but she's been abducted because of me. I just need to know if you recall anyone following us out?"

She's silent for a moment. "No. I don't recall. I'll ask the night guards. Wait."

After a minute, she comes back. "No. They said no one left after you for a good hour."

My shoulders droop, feeling heavy, and I sit on the table behind me. "Okay. Well, thanks for asking."

My sister is quiet for long enough that I think she has hung up on me, but then she adds, "You get too close, Everleigh. Just let her go. Move on. It's safer that way."

I let out a sad sigh, knowing she means well in her own way. "Thanks, Clara."

"Sure," she says. Then the phone goes dead.

I walk back to Tessa and Alaric, and they stop talking when I get close.

"No one left the club for around an hour after we did. I don't think it was there."

Alaric lets out a frustrated growl, and Tessa looks at him with surprise.

"Are you all right, Alaric?" she asks.

"Fine. Fine. We must be missing something, though. This case is driving me up the wall. Whoever is doing this certainly knows how to keep us in the dark."

Feeling his frustration, I can't help but reach out and rest my hand on his shoulder, trying to offer a little of the support he gave me earlier.

"Well, we do have one lead still," I say, a little uncertainly. "Evan."

Alaric shakes his head. "Sorry, Everleigh. I did go back and work on him again and we couldn't get anything more. He's turned out to be a bit of a dead end."

The darker side of me flickers awake, the same part that ate up the sight of Alaric inflicting violence, and a horribly wonderful idea comes to mind. My angelic side feels nauseous. The demonic part of me is thrilled. And like every time this happens, my heart begins to race, and I feel the red pushing to shine through my eyes. "You haven't let me try yet."

Tessa chuckles. "Alaric is pretty thorough on the torture front, no matter how much he hates it. Do you really think you could do any better?"

Alaric's eyes flash to Tessa's in warning, and he pinches his lips together tight enough that the color disappears.

I let the red come to the surface, the shine reflecting off the computer screens nearby. "I have a unique... option... that might help." I look imploringly at Alaric and try to pull my smile back, certain I look half-crazed. "Can I try?"

Tessa shifts back in her chair in shock.

Alaric looks at me speculatively for a few seconds, then says, "We're at a dead end up here. You can try."

Yes! My turn.

Alaric has me wait in the interrogation room while he goes and fetches Evan.

The angelic part of me, the part my mother would be proud of if she were still here, hates my demonic power. The cost is rarely worth the reward, but not this time. Henry is worth it. Raine is worth it. So instead of pushing away the demon in me, I embrace her in a way I rarely do.

My insides fill with the heat of the Hells, of hate, of revenge. Of my father's legacy. The power that was his to wield. That came to me when he died. I breathe it in.

When the door opens, a wild laugh escapes me, and I turn to look at both Alaric and Evan. One I'd like to taste. One I'd like to kill. One predator. One prey.

I grin ferally and take a step forward.

Evan jerks to a halt, backing into Alaric, and I let loose a cackle.

"Come in, little mouse. Take a seat."

Alaric manages to keep his face mostly neutral, and I offer him a sultry wink.

I feel the angelic side of me try to resist the overt behavior and I lock it down, focusing back on my prey. The one who has the answer to our question.

Alaric shoves Evan into the chair and secures him in place before stepping out of my way, clearly unsure of what I'm doing since I didn't really explain.

I stalk towards Evan, who's pointlessly trying to push back a chair that's bolted into the cement floor.

"Tsk. Tsk. Tsk."

I lean close to his face, eating up the fear he's exuding, and see the red glow of my eyes reflect in his.

"I'm going to give you one chance now. My friends have been taken. Since my wolf wasn't able to get your boss's name from you, I'm willing to bet you don't actually know it."

His eyes widen, shock beating out the fear for just a moment.

"Oh, yes. A predator your boss is. He won't give himself away so easily. But you do know some things. Tell me where my friends might have been taken."

Evan opens his mouth but has to close it and wet it with saliva so he can speak. "I... I... can't tell you anything. If I do, I'm as good as dead."

I pout at him and lean forward to whisper in his ear.

"There are things worse than being dead, little mouse. I'm feeling generous. Last chance. Tell me the locations he might be keeping them."

I lean back and tilt my head to the side as I lock my eyes with his. He swallows audibly and shakes his head a fraction in each direction.

I grin with my teeth bared.

"Wrong answer."

I place one hand on each of his shoulders and move in until I can see into the depths of his pupils. I pull on the flames of the Hells inside me and bring them to the surface. I send them out of my eyes and into his. All his fears dance before me, and I pick the worst—his fear of snakes—and begin to weave it, then I force it into his mind.

Evan is in a small, deep well. Snakes slither down from the top. Up from the floors. Out of the holes in the stone walls. Snakes as wide as his arms. Eyes red like mine. Red venom and blood dripping from their fangs as they move closer. Their hunger fills his mind. He knows they want to taste him. To eat him. To consume him.

"Get them off me! Make it stop!" His voice is hoarse. Breaths shallow. Body convulsing. He smells like piss.

I pull back the nightmare just enough to get his attention.

"Are you ready to tell me, little mouse? Or are you ready to be eaten?"

"No! Stop. Stop! I'll tell you. All the places. Anything you want. Just stop. Stop. Please!" he begs in strangled gasps.

I withdraw the nightmare completely, though I know from experience that he'll see this particular scene every time he closes his eyes for a long time to come. Will feel it all as if it's real. A part of the gift. The curse.

He looks at me and immediately averts his gaze and finds Alaric. "Not her. You. Make her go." His voice turns to a pathetic whine. "Please. Make her go!"

I laugh and look at Alaric. Even his expressionless face isn't enough to pull the wind from my sails. The thought crosses my mind briefly to see if I can make him tell me what it is he really thinks, but the angelic side of me is there again, resisting, pulling back control.

Alaric seems to sense something is changing and stands up.

I look directly at Evan's back, sure he can feel it from the tremor that runs through him. My demonic side speaks one last time before I shove it back down.

"Start talking. Now. Or I'll be back, and the second time won't be so nice."

Then I charge out the door.

By the time Alaric joins me, I'm mostly back to myself. But I feel it—the change, the little piece of my soul that has darkened from using my father's power. The more times I use it, the darker my soul becomes, the lightness tarnished, my demonic side a little louder, more present.

"You good?" Alaric asks quietly.

I blow a breath out through my nose. "As well as I'm going to be right now. Please tell me you got something."

He smiles tightly. "I got something. I've already sent the locations to Tessa and the twins. I expect they'll know something by the time we make it up there. Are you ready?"

"Good. Okay. Let's go."

I follow him up and almost collapse in relief when Tessa calls, "We've got them. There's CCTV footage of them being carried into one of the buildings in the warehouse district I just linked to your phone, Alaric."

"Well done. Okay. Send anyone you can round up, Tessa." He turns to me. "Let's go get your friends back."

My little spark of hope blooms, and I rush out to the car immediately, determined to rescue my friends.

We're down the block from what appears to be a deserted collection of warehouses, but Alaric assures me the vampires are close by.

"The team will be here any minute now. Trust me. We should wait. Going in with only the two of us will be worse for Raine and Henry, okay?"

Impatient to get to my friends but willing to wait a couple of minutes longer in the hopes that we can get them out alive, I pace back and forth between buildings, moderately weighed down by the weapons we stacked on from Alaric's trunk.

I pause when a bulky guy walks over to us, followed by a woman and another man. The bulky guy has camo pants, a crew cut, and a wolf tattoo on his neck. No guesses required. The woman has the telltale beauty of the fae. And the final piece of our puzzle is clearly a mage. His gray hair tells me he's older than the usual mage, whose lives seem to inexplicably run short, and his bulky jacket suggests he's well stocked.

But still.

I look at Alaric. "*This* is the team. *Really?*" I turn my head back to them. "No offense, but Tessa said we're looking at pretty high numbers here."

The mage frowns down at me. "We don't need numbers, girl. We need power and strength and brains."

"Besides," adds the other werewolf, "this job doesn't exactly draw in a crowd. Be grateful you got another three of us here. It's practically unheard of."

"Enough," Alaric says. "We need to move. Everleigh and I will take the front door. You lot take the back and sides as you like. You all got the pictures of who we're here for?"

I love a man in charge... When I say so.

They nod and walk away, not bothering to introduce themselves, and I decide now isn't the time to worry about names. It's time to rescue my friends.

We approach the front of the warehouse directly, and Alaric uses his crossbow to stake the vamp out the front as soon as his body is facing ours. We don't bother taking the quiet approach, and we watch as the body falls with a thud.

In a second, we're past the guard, and Alaric flings the door wide and steps in. I follow, slamming the door shut behind me, and immediately release my wings from the ether. The golden-white lights the room, and my racing heart jumps to a dangerous speed. There are at least fifteen vamps here.

They take a collective step toward us, but then three other doors burst open, and are quickly closed.

There's a moment where the vampires freeze, unsure of where to go. The enforcement team and I use their indecision to attack. I fly towards the roof armed with my canister of liquid silver, set to spray rather than stream, aiming for pain and distraction over death to give everyone a better chance. From the air, I see the mage throw a flaming potion from the left of the room, the wolf transforms on the right, and the fae woman flies forward, brandishing a silver-tipped staff. Below me, there's the whoosh of another stake flying through the air. Several thuds sound as bodies hit the ground, and the room becomes a war zone.

I shoot the silver spray over the vampires closest to the mage, knowing it won't damage him. The screeches and battle cries are deafening.

No longer able to get a clear view of the chaos, I land close to Alaric and pull out my wooden stake. Two vampires run at me at once, a female, all claws and fangs, while the male has a solid chain. I slice toward the female, connecting with her arm, and make a quick sidestep to avoid the chain. It still hits the side of my leg, and I know it's going to bruise at the very least.

Fucking vampire speed.

The female vamp comes straight at me, claws out. I lift my left hand up as though I'm trying to defend my neck. She takes the bait, and bites down. Ignoring the sharp, hot pain, I thrust the stake straight up into her heart. She stills immediately, held up only by her teeth in my arm. I shove her back into the male vamp who is almost on top of us, causing him to catch her for a split second. Before I have a chance to do anything, the vamp is on fire, courtesy of the mage, and then his head is on the floor, with thanks to the fae warrior.

With a quick glance, I can see the vamp numbers are dropping quickly. I also spot Raine and Henry lying on a second-floor landing at the rear of the warehouse. I use my wings to take to the air again and hear a shout from below.

"Everleigh! Stop!"

It's Alaric, but he's too slow. I try to suppress a scream as two spear-like weapons shoot through my wings. They're attached to ropes that pull tight and lock me in place. The pain is excruciating, and I can't move. Then, just as suddenly, the taut ropes slacken, and I land as gently as I can back onto the ground, away from the melee. I vaguely notice that even fewer vamps are now standing as I breathe through the agony.

I draw my bleeding, damaged wings in close, grab one of the ribbed weapons, and rip it out, screaming as I do. I heave in rapid breaths as I let the natural healing take over. Not paying enough attention, I shriek when my left wing is yanked by the large rope attached to the spear.

I pull out two vials of powdered silver and peg the first one at the vamp holding the rope. As expected, he dodges the first, giving me a crazed grin, but the second one he never saw coming smashes at his feet, causing the silver to fly up and stick to all of his exposed skin.

"You hybrid bitch. You'll pay for that!"

Needing half a second more to recover, I hold my hand up and gesture for him to come closer. He can't help himself.

The second he's close enough, I pull the short sword Alaric gave me from its sheath and bring it up in an arc, taking his head off his shoulders. It drops with a dull thud to the concrete floor. Blood spatters around it and then oozes slowly from the wound.

Around the room, it's down to one on one, so I take the chance to pull the other spear out of my wing and watch more closely as the other vampires are put down. I heal while still gasping for air.

In less than a minute, the last of the vampires have been killed. I look up to the landing and see that the vamp that was there is now gone. A door at the back of the second level is wide open.

I turn to Alaric and point at the open door. "I'm fairly sure one escaped."

He looks at his team. "Is anyone up for a hunt?"

The fae woman looks at the two men on either side of her, bleeding in several places, and she snorts. "Men." Then in a puff of fluorescent green light, she transforms into a falcon and flies out the open door.

The other enforcers mutter between themselves for a moment, then the mage calls out to Alaric, "We're going to follow in the car. Just in case Perri needs us."

I switch off listening to whatever they are saying, pull my now aching wings back to the ether to finish healing, and head to the stairs. At the top, Henry and Raine are trussed up in chains and cuffed to a metal ring attached to the floor. I see a little blood staining their heads and the floor they're lying on, and they have bruises all over them. I know the bruises and blood will heal. As long as they're both alive.

I move slowly closer, my heartbeat erratic, hesitant to learn the truth. Halfway there, footsteps sound behind me, and I spin, sword out. It's just Alaric, a little bloodied and bruised, but somehow still mouth-wateringly handsome. I give him a quick smile as I drop the sword to my side and move to my friends. As soon as I'm within a few meters, the relief I feel is so strong, I almost vomit.

They're both breathing—Henry twice as fast as Raine—which means they're both still alive.

I rush the last couple of steps and drop to their sides. With Alaric's help, we remove the chains tying them down. Raine starts healing almost instantly, and within a minute, she sits up. I crash into her, giving her a tight squeeze.

"I'm so, so, so sorry, Raine."

She hugs me back so tightly it hurts, but in a way, it's still not tight enough. I sit back when she relaxes her hold on me and look at Henry.

"Is he...?" Raine pauses and looks at me. "Will he be okay?"

"I hope so. His breathing is okay. I think we just need to get him to a doctor."

Without being asked, Alaric lifts Henry as though he weighs nothing. I smile gratefully and, overwhelmed with gratitude, I lean forward and kiss Alaric on the cheek.

Heat rushes to my face immediately. "I, uh." I look away for a second, and back to him. "Thank you."

He nods, eyes heated, then turns and walks towards the stairs.

Raine bumps her shoulder into mine, grinning like a maniac despite what's just happened, and I can't help returning her smile.

Until my phone buzzes in my pocket.

Unknown: Well done on retrieving your little chess pieces. But I hope you don't think our game is over just yet.

SACRIFICES

THE NEXT NIGHT, RAINE, Alaric, and I sit around Henry's hospital bed sharing Chinese takeout—Henry's favorite.

"I know I've already said it fifty times to you, Raine, but I'm so sorry this happened." I look at Henry, whose head is wrapped in a bandage, and my nausea continues to swirl. "I understand if you'd both rather steer clear of me." I laugh mockingly. "Hey, *I'd* steer clear of me if I could."

I can feel the disapproval exuding from Alaric in waves, but I do my best to ignore it and focus on my friends.

Raine huffs. "You know my opinion, Ev. It isn't your fault, and I'm certainly not staying away. You're my friend."

Henry reaches out his hand, and I lean forward so I can take it.

"Raine is right. No one here blames you, and none of us want you out of our lives." He chuckles softly. "You're stuck with us."

I harrumph at them. "You're both too stubborn. Being my friend isn't worth the cost. We got you back this time, but what if next time..." I swallow past the lump in my throat. "What if next time we don't?"

Raine stands, walks around Henry's bed, and hugs me tightly. "Henry's right. You're stuck with us. You have our back, and we have yours. That's just the way it is."

A lightness fills me, knowing I have others who truly care for me outside of my family. Real friends.

Raine goes back to her seat, then looks at Alaric and gives him a tight smile. "I already know I'm not going to be much help, but I assume you want to ask us some questions?"

"Yes," he says. "Can either of you remember *anything* that happened?"

Raine gestures at Henry for him to go first. I sense her frustration. She's spent the last twenty-four hours trying to remember something and keeps coming up empty.

Henry scrunches his eyes as though he is visibly trying to think. "We booked a taxi to pick us up, like we told Ev. For *some reason—*" He rolls his eyes, though appears to immediately regret it as he grabs his head "—they wanted to pick us up a little down the street. I didn't think much of it, except that it was annoying. When we were almost at the pickup point, I remember a massive pain in the back of my head, and then everything went black. The next thing I can recall is being here in the hospital." He looks between Alaric and me. "Sorry, guys. I wish I could be of more help."

I gently pat Henry on the shoulder. "Hey, it's hardly your fault someone knocked you out."

His mouth pulls up at the sides, but it doesn't bring out his dimples.

Raine huffs with irritation. "It's the same for me. Nothing different. I don't remember anyone watching us or following us or anything remotely suspicious."

Alaric rubs a hand across his brow, and I notice how tired he looks. It makes me wonder if he's been sleeping. *I should ask later.*

After a moment, he perks up, sitting taller in his chair. He opens his mouth to say something, then looks at me and closes it, before twisting his lips to the left.

He obviously has something to say that I'm not going to like. I raise my brows and wait.

Alaric snorts indelicately. "I know you won't like this idea, and it wouldn't work with Henry, but we could visit one of the mind witches with Raine. To see if they can scan her memory." His voice fades out at the end when he sees the fury on my face.

"No bloody way."

"Hold on!" Raine says. "I want to help."

I glare at Alaric but speak to Raine. "What he's talking about is dangerous, not to mention excruciatingly painful."

Alaric has the good sense to look a little abashed, but the damage has already been done.

"I should be the one who gets to decide," says Raine. "We need something solid to stop this guy." She looks at me with big, puppy-dog eyes. "I don't want this to happen to any more people or for anyone else to get hurt if I can do something to prevent it."

I growl in frustration and pin Alaric with an angry stare. "You better have someone fantastic on retainer who isn't going to do any damage."

"Yay!" Raine claps her hands. "Thank you, Ev. You're the best."

I sit back and fold my arms, lips pursed. "Don't be so happy. It's going to bloody hurt."

I sit silently in Alaric's car with him and Raine as we drive out of the city. Worries about the potential damage of using a mind witch swirl around in my head. The best-case scenario for Raine is that it will hurt like a bitch. Worst-case? Brain damage for the rest of her immortal life. *No big deal, right?*

Knowing it was her choice isn't helping me to feel any better about the situation, so I sit silently in my own imaginary anxious bubble, a mess of nerves and fears.

"We'll be there in ten minutes," Alaric says, breaking a silence so dense that I jump a little and hear Raine do the same.

I sigh and decide to try one last time. Turning around, I lock my gaze with Raine's, making sure she can see how serious I am.

"Are you sure you don't want to reconsider? No one will think less of you. We can find another way. A better and safer way. I care about you. I don't want you to get hurt again."

Raine leans forward and places her hand on my cheek. "I know, Ev. I understand. But my life changed in a way I never would have wanted it to, and it's scary. Doing this might stop it from happening to anyone else. How many people have lost their families and loved ones already because of this guy? There hasn't been enough progress." She leans forward, and whispers fiercely in my ear, "I can do this. And I'll be okay. I promise."

I look at my new supernatural friend—something I never thought I'd have after the last seventy years—and feel heavy, weighed down almost. Twenty-seven years probably feels like a lot to a human, but Raine's immortal life will be longer than she can understand right now. Despite feelings she can't understand, I need to let her have this.

Alaric remains silent as he pulls the car into a long, paved driveway by the ocean. At the end is a small stone cottage set in a forest of native plants and trees. If you like plants, I imagine it would be quite a haven.

We get out of the car, and Raine and I fall behind Alaric. She grasps my hand in hers and squeezes, smiling at me reassuringly. I do my best to return her expression with just as much love and care.

Before we reach the cottage door, it swings open, revealing a small, old lady. She wears an old-fashioned, pale blue dress, and her gray hair falls softly on her shoulders. She smiles at us with several missing teeth.

"Well, come on in, dears. Let's leave the sea breeze outside."

We trail behind her, closing the door as we walk through. Down the end of a long, buttery-yellow hallway is a sitting room that looks like it could belong to any little old woman.

"So." She looks at Alaric. "My fee first, if you please." The small woman winks at Raine and me. "Inflation, you know."

I smile despite myself when I see Raine nodding emphatically at the witch.

Alaric hands over a pile of gift cards, each worth a thousand dollars, to the different stores she'd demanded of him earlier. She takes them from him gleefully, walks over to a small cabinet, and mutters words that cause goose pimples to rise all over me. Then she stuffs them in, slams it shut, and returns to us.

"Uh, excuse me," says Raine, who looks awkwardly between us all for a moment, "but what is your name?"

I cringe, having forgotten to tell her that some of the older witches prefer to keep such powerful things as names hidden. And that asking can be considered rather insulting.

The little old lady cackles. "New, aren't we, deary? You can call me... Glinda."

Raine laughs back. "Like Glinda, the good witch from *The Wizard of Oz*?"

The small lady grins. "Right you are, deary. Now"—she points to a single, powder blue lounge with daisies on it at the edge of the room—"take a seat."

Raine hesitates, looking unsure.

It's my turn to be a better friend. I hug her, then whisper in her ear, "You're brave and you are selfless, Raine. This will help a lot of people. And I'm here for you, okay? You've got this."

Raine pulls back from me, determination evident in her posture. "I've got this," she repeats. Then she walks over to the chair and sits.

"Arms up on the sides there, deary. That's the way."

Without warning, cuffs shoot out of the once-innocuous-looking armchair and lock her into place. I step forward, ready to protest, but Alaric grabs my wrist, not tight enough to stop me but enough to get my attention.

"It's okay. It's just so Raine doesn't move. Or... Glinda"—he shakes his head— "will have to start again."

I watch the little old lady closely as she stands behind the chair and places her wrinkled hands on each side of Raine's head.

"When we discussed payment, Alaric told me what we are searching for. So, if you just think back to right before you were taken, I can follow through from there."

"I can do that," Raine says.

The witch begins muttering words in an ancient tongue I don't understand, and my heart begins to race as fear for Raine overpowers my logical thoughts. I wrap my hand around Alaric's and watch in horror as Raine's mouth opens with a silent scream.

The witch continues to chant.

Louder.

Softer.

Louder again.

Raine's eyes shoot open. Bloody tears stream down her face. But still, no sound comes out. Filled with worry and guilt, I squeeze Alaric's arm and feel tears of my own mirror my friend's.

Alaric wraps his arm around me and pulls me in. My gaze flickers to him for a split second, but he's watching Raine—and the little old witch.

She squeezes harder. Chants louder. Then stops.

The manacles retreat into the armchair, and I rush to catch Raine as she flops forward. I hold her close while the witch sits on the sofa and takes a long drink.

After a few moments, Raine comes to. Alaric hands me a couple of tissues, which I use to clean her face.

"Are you all right?" I ask her quietly.

Raine smiles at me weakly, looking exhausted. "I'll be okay," she promises before she asks her own question of the lady who was inside her mind. "Did you find anything?"

The witch looks around the room at each of us, then back to Raine, the side of her mouth pulling up. "I did say you could call me Glinda, didn't I?" She laughs at her own joke, then asks casually, as if she weren't dropping the most crucial piece of information in our case, "Does the name Silas mean anything to you?" Shock at the discovery resonates through our little group as we say thanks to the old witch and make our way outside.

Alaric drives us back down the street before pulling over to make a call to Orpheus.

Immediately after he delivers the news, he holds the phone at arm's length to get some distance from the roar on the other end.

"What in the hells do you mean... Silas? He's one of the oldest among us. He's been a loyal supporter during my entire leadership in this position. Why in the bloody hells would he do this to me?"

The yelling becomes muffled for a moment, and I glance at Alaric, who looks utterly bored with the vampire king's shouting about his political problems.

When there is silence for long enough, Alaric brings the phone back. "What are your instructions?"

Something made of glass smashes on the other end of the call, and then Orpheus is back. "Bring him in. I can't be seen doing it. This is going to be a nightmare."

I pipe up, "What do you mean, 'bring him in?' Do you really think he's going to just jump in the car when he's gone to this much trouble?"

"No," he snaps, then hangs up.

Alaric and I stand outside the gates to Silas's house, and I can't help but stare at the shifter with wide eyes.

"Do you really think going in here to get this, like, thousands-of-years-old vamp, is a good idea? Surely the Council should take care of this one? Or at least Orpheus could?"

The rumble vibrates in Alaric's chest. "No, I don't think it's reasonable. And like I already said, you should have stayed at home with Raine."

"You're kidding me, right?" I put my hands on my hips, and then, feeling childish, immediately pull them back down. "You, by yourself, with zero help. What happened to the other enforcers?"

He growls at me quietly. "They're busy. Just go home. It's safer that way."

I ignore him and walk up to the gate.

"What in the hellish realms are you doing?"

"I'm going in. Standing here isn't achieving anything."

"What? Right up to the front door?"

I huff out a breath. "Couldn't hurt to ask. Something tells me he's expecting us anyway since he's literally been sending me texts."

"No. Come on. We're going up the side. Stay with me."

"Sure," I mutter. *Stay with Mr. Moody.*

When we get close enough to the front door, I see it's already wide open, and my stomach knots tighter. It suddenly feels harder to take a full breath.

"I told you he knows," I hiss.

Worry flashes over Alaric's features, his brows drawn down and his lips pulled into his teeth.

"Okay," he says, then takes a deep breath. "Let's go to the front door. But to be clear, I don't like this."

"Neither do I. I hope Orpheus loses his stupid crown for making us do this so he can save political face."

Inside the door, a male voice calls out, "Check."

The word echoes around the large room *and* through my head. I try to force some confidence into my posture by rolling my shoulders back and standing a little taller.

"At least we know we're in the right place. Come on," I say to Alaric, before raising my voice to address the ancient vampire. "I don't suppose you'd like to just come down to the Council building with us, Silas?"

"Perhaps." He laughs. "If you can make me."

The echoes of his taunting voice make it impossible to figure out where he is. I point to my own chest, then Alaric's, then to the opposite ends of the room.

He frowns at me, then nods, but points to a stake in my belt. We pull out our stakes simultaneously and head in different directions.

I move into a scarcely decorated entertaining parlor on the right and through to a long, dark hall.

Silas's laughter echoes down the hall. Loud, then soft.

I take careful steps, sticking close to the wall. Following the laughter until I reach a single, closed door.

I feel a breath on my neck. I turn.

Empty space.

I shiver, heart pounding, and turn back to the door. I push it open, and it creaks so loudly, I feel the sound ricochet through my insides. If Silas didn't know where I was before, he does now. The room is pitch black when I reach in to find the lightswitch. It's dead.

Half scared and half impatient, I step in and pull my wings from the ether. Their golden-white glow fills the room. It's lined with mirrors but completely bare in the center.

What in all the layers of the hells is wrong with this guy?

Footsteps sound, and I turn immediately to the door, stake raised.

When Alaric enters, I sag a little in relief.

"Did you find any—"

Alaric swings his stake at me, and I stumble back, only just avoiding the blow. I try to talk, but he's on me again. He swings. I duck.

A shadow appears in the doorway. That wicked laugh is back.

Alaric's stake slices through my arm, and I hiss. Trying not to get stabbed when you aren't willing to stab back is difficult.

"Let him go, you bloody coward," I yell at Silas, who has stopped just inside the door so he can watch me try not to hurt Alaric.

"Oh, come now." He chuckles. "This is far more amusing for our little game. Just killing you both would be too easy."

I fly back a few feet, trying to get more space, but Alaric is on me again. *I need to do something or he's going to kill me.*

I turn my stake upside down and start hitting back with the blunt end.

"I suppose I should have known you'd be—" I kick Alaric's leg out from under him and try to smack him in the temple, but he rolls away "—too scared to fight on your own."

Silas stops laughing and a hot slice of pleasure runs through me. It quickly fades when I notice him stalking towards me.

Between blinks, Raine, who was meant to be at home, charges in, and my heart stutters. She launches a whole armchair from somewhere in the house at Silas's back.

Sensing it with a split second to spare, he swings around and bats it out of the way with both hands. He lets out a primal snarl. A half-glance at Alaric shows me he's frozen in place with Silas's distraction. I turn back to my friend.

Raine pulls out one of Silas's decorative swords from her belt and rushes forward to attack him.

She cringes and turns to the side as he collides with her, sending her flying into a mirror. Shards fly everywhere. Raine crashes to the floor with a groan, and I cringe with her in sympathy.

Silas stalks towards her, crushing glass exaggerating each step he takes.

I'm about to rush over to save Raine when a tap on the shoulder nearly makes me jump out of my skin. Alaric has his finger to his mouth.

Relief flushes through my system, a small balm in the chaos. *He's back. Thank God for Raine. I could kiss her right now.*

I look quickly back to the fight and notice the walls are mostly bare concrete now. Silas can't see us.

I turn back to Alaric with a plan and see he's a step ahead of me. His protective gloves are on, and he shoves a silver canister into my hand.

He's holding the net. He points at the melee, then rushes towards the door.

Raine screeches at Silas, and I whip around to look at them.

He's pulling her up by the hair.

"Let me go!" She kicks wildly at him, thrashing until she's too hard to hold.

Once Alaric is in position, I run at Silas, not bothering to quieten my steps. When I'm two meters away, I make a loud battle cry.

He drops Raine, and spins straight to me, somehow holding her sword, and I spray the stream of liquid silver at his face, as he stabs the blade into my stomach.

I drop the canister as white-hot pain flares through me and Silas hisses and grabs his face.

It's enough.

Alaric tosses the silver net over him. He falls to the ground with the sound and scent of sizzling flesh filling the room.

I walk over to him, clutching my side, as I wait for my healing abilities to finish doing their job. Looking down at his feral face, my eyes flaring red, I bare my teeth.

"Check. Mate."

LEGACY

ALARIC, RAINE, AND I sit in the meeting room of the Council of the Accord. Except this time, we're not front and center. Silas is.

The Council looks at him, expressions ranging from disapproving to bored, with the exception of Orpheus, who looks equally outraged and confused.

Orpheus opens his mouth to speak, and Silas cuts him off.

"Why is it that I'm here instead of before the vampire council? I have little interest in the opinions of those in this room."

Nicon can't seem to help the smirk that grows on his face, but not because of what Silas has said. He watches Orpheus, who looks like he's going to explode with his flushed cheeks and bulging eyes.

Perhaps sensing the potential chaos, Octavia, the high witch, intervenes. "While I can understand your lack of care for those in this room, you are here because your crimes have caused quite the issue for the entire supernatural community. Many across the Council departments have needed to work harder to clean up your messes and to keep our existence in check."

Silas looks uninterested. He turns back to Orpheus, but this time, Orpheus manages to speak first.

"Why? Just... *why*? You have been a supporter for as long as I have been king. Why would you do this?"

He shrugs nonchalantly. "Legacy."

Orpheus drops his chin and arches his brows. His tone is pure disbelief. "Legacy?"

"I find I've had quite enough of this... existence. If you can call it that. I wanted some progeny to carry on after I'm gone."

Orpheus's voice becomes strained. "And you couldn't just follow the process like everyone else?"

"Certainly not. I haven't been on this earth for so long just so I can wait in line in an office to get permission for something that is my right as a creature of the darkness. Nor did I have any interest in limiting my options."

Nicon is grinning now, and even Iridessa looks somewhat amused. I get the impression based on who they each watch that their motivations differ greatly. To be fair, Iridessa has been around longer than most in the room and can likely relate to what Silas is saying.

Orpheus looks defeated and waves towards the rest of the Council.

Iridessa picks up a glass of liquid from beside her and swirls it around, gaining everyone's attention. "While I appreciate the desire to leave behind a legacy, you have blatantly flouted the rules and almost caused exposure before it is time."

Others in the Council shift uncomfortably at her choice of words.

She taps her nails on the glass, then looks at Silas with big doe-eyes full of fake remorse. "You have a few progenies now. I think it's time you went to sleep."

I watch each of the Council members in turn. None speak but all nod, except for Orpheus. Instead, he stands and lets out a long sigh, then walks to Silas, who still looks unmoved by the decision in the room.

"May you finally have the rest you so desire. *Somnum bene.* Sleep well, friend."

Silas bows his head at Orpheus, then raises his chin, eyes closed, peaceful despite the chaos he's caused.

A silver sword slashes through the air so quickly, I almost don't see it. One moment Silas has his head. The next, it's on the floor.

Raine gives a little squeal beside me, and I reach out to her. She grabs my hand and squeezes it tight before forcing a smile and letting me go. I try to subtly stretch out my hand, so she doesn't know it hurts.

While I was supporting Raine, Orpheus managed to return his sword to wherever it was sheathed and take his seat again. In the center of the room, Silas's head, body, and the chair he was resting on are gone. I blink in confusion, sure I hadn't looked away for that long.

Iridessa raises her hand towards the roof and clicks. Three chairs appear to replace the one that has been taken away. *Ah, magic*. Sometimes I forget some of the fae have such a talent, and my mind flashes to the sound of my father telling me I would do well not to forget such a thing.

Raphael, silent until now, stands. He looks at the three of us. "Please. Come and sit."

I shrug, figuring we're in this room for more reasons than to watch Silas's punishment after helping solve this case. I lead the way over to the chairs with Raine close by my side and Alaric behind us. Once we sit, I look at Raphael and wait.

"First, we thank each of you for putting an end to the threat that Silas posed to the supernatural community. It was a hard-earned victory, and one not without sacrifice."

Raphael stares at me as he says the last part, and my insides chill.

Can he see the stain on my essence from using the power my father left for me?

Even with no judgment in his eyes, my knowing that he might have guessed is enough. It's a secret I don't want to share, especially when I don't know what it might mean.

I do my best to remain indifferent on the outside, but inside, I can feel myself unraveling with the uncertainty.

Alaric nods in acknowledgment beside me, prompting me to do the same. Being disrespectful won't help in this meeting.

Raine copies both of us.

Come on, Ev. Focus. For your friend.

My lips curve up a touch and I pull them back down quickly. Now isn't the time to be happy about having a friend.

"Everleigh, daughter of Estelle."

"Yes?"

"While rare, the Council would like to offer you a deal."

I shift in my seat, unsure where this is going.

"After this case was solved, we discussed the potential benefit of having someone with angelic powers working with the enforcers. I can provide you with a talisman of sorts that will assist in channeling your visions towards certain cases should it be needed."

Alaric lets out a low growl, and I stare at him with wide eyes.

"Alaric! Control yourself," Conall barks, unimpressed by his underling's outburst in front of his peers.

I turn to the front, a little confused by Alaric's objection. "I don't want to do that job. I have a job already. They're waiting for me to come back."

"Your job with the humans?" the head mage inquires, his voice dismissive.

"Yes." I try to make sure my tone leaves no room for discussion, but I know they won't care.

"Be that as it may," Raphael responds, "the Council wishes to offer you a deal. If you agree to work for the enforcement department, I will agree to reduce your fealty sentence to seventy-five years."

I shake my head. "Twenty-five years is nothing."

Nicon grins, an excited light in his eyes, then blurts, "Fifty years!"

Several of the others frown at the demon, who is acting like he's joined a game show, while Raphael simply stares for a moment, then turns back to me. "Would you accept fifty years?"

I pause to think, knowing I don't truly care about the years but about those important to me. I look at Raine and see her encouraging smile. Before I can say anything, Alaric grabs my arm, drawing my attention back to him.

"Don't, Everleigh. This job... it... Just don't. Please." He looks at me and allows some of the pain he must feel on the inside to come out, and it hurts my heart.

I place my hand lightly on his. "Please, Alaric. I need you to trust me here."

Sorrow fills his eyes, and he withdraws his hand, adding a bigger ache to my heart. I know deep within myself that I can fix things with him later, but this is the only chance I will get to make a deal to help Raine.

I meet Raphael's eyes and make a counteroffer. "I will accept the fifty years, but only on one condition."

Nicon leans forward, a maniacal smile lighting his face, while the Arch Mage snorts derisively.

"And what is that?" Raphael asks, a hint of curiosity in his otherwise neutral tone.

"You allowed me to keep Raine under my care during her initial transition period in exchange for me assisting with this case. My condition is that I take on the role of being her carer on a permanent basis." I sit back and wait, keeping very still.

Solomon interjects almost immediately. "That is unheard of. Everleigh is not a vampire. She can hardly take on the role of master."

Nicon turns to the mage. "I'm willing to make a wager on it. Interested?"

"You're a fool, demon," he spits back, irritation getting the better of him.

Conall leans back in his chair and crosses his right ankle over his left knee. "I feel like the only one who can really make this concession is Orpheus. Can it be done? Of course. Should it be done?" He pierces the vampire with a hard stare. "That is up to you."

Anticipation tightens my chest. All he has to do is say no, and it's over. I'll need to find a new way to keep Raine with me. I would not allow her to be dropped into the ranks of an unknown vampire master.

Orpheus contemplates the werewolf king's words for what feels like an eternity but is only about thirty seconds. "Given the fledgling's control, and Miss Cole ensuring she has not killed any humans thus far, I am willing to assist the Council in this matter and agree to the concession."

Always with the politics.

"Very well," Raphael says. "It seems we have a deal. Fifty years of fealty to be served as a Council enforcer, and the vampire Raine is permanently assigned to you. Agreed?"

My heart races. I feel like I'm flying.

This couldn't have gone better.

"Agreed," I say, as levelly as I can manage with joy bursting in my chest.

Nicon bounds up from his seat the moment Raphael sits down, mischief written all over his face. "Excellent. As the Council member doomed to be responsible for the enforcement department, I volunteer Alaric as Everleigh's guide and partner during the process."

Conall groans from his reclined position and puts his head into his hand.

Alaric and I look at each other, and despite his strained expression, I can't help but wonder if it *did* just get better.

After the meeting, Alaric takes us home. When he pulls up out the front of the building, I look at Raine, then quickly dart a glance towards Alaric. She immediately gets the idea and mouths the word "later" with a wink.

"I'll meet you upstairs, Ev. Thanks, Alaric. I'm looking forward to seeing you around more." She gives him a cheeky grin and jumps out of the car, swinging the door shut behind her.

He turns to me, expression raw. "You shouldn't have done it, Everleigh."

I meet his eyes and say gently, "I get the impression that there's a lot more to this job than what happened in this one case. Even seeing the other enforcers, I got a sense of heaviness."

Alaric nods. "This case, in some ways, was milder, but mostly it's that this job is almost impossible if you have anyone you care about. I know you took this job to help Raine, to protect her. But having her in your life will become a liability. A risk. She'll always be in danger because of your connection."

A heaviness builds in my chest again, pulling more of the joy away from keeping Raine close by. "I understand, and I know you don't agree, but I've made this decision so I'm going to do my best to keep her safe. I'll find a way. I'll train her in self-defense so she can protect herself better when I'm not there."

"I'm sure you will, Everleigh. I just... It's going to be hard, okay?"

"All right," I say softly. I grab the door handle but pause and turn back. "I know Nicon assigned you to guide me in the job but, I mean, if you'd rather not, I could try and ask him to get someone else to—"

"No!" He sits up straighter, a flush reaching his sharp cheekbones. "Sorry. No, not unless you're not comfortable with it. I... working with me will be safest."

I smile softly, feeling a warmth along my collarbone. "Okay, well, I'll see you on Monday?"

He nods, a smile pulling up at his lips despite the remnants of sadness in his gaze. "Monday," he agrees.

My heart melts at his rare smile, and an eagerness I never suspected about starting the job hits me hard.

The next afternoon, Raine and I walk down the street, close to the supe bar we previously visited. We somehow end up wearing matching yellow sundresses that swish around in the light breeze that keeps the summer heat from cooking us as we walk.

"So, where to *Master*?" She bumps into me good-naturedly, grinning like a kid who just had all her birthday wishes come true.

I snort and laugh. "Cut it out. I'm not your master."

"Sure, sure," she teases. "Where are we heading though, Miss Secretive?"

I look around, sure now that we've crossed the ward boundary that keeps the humans away, and I come to a stop.

I reach out my hands and Raine takes them, curiosity plain on her face.

"I have an idea, but you can say no if you want to, okay?" My heart races a little, nervous to hear what she thinks of my plan.

"Of course," she says seriously. "What is it?"

"I know I'm not a vampire, and I'm never going to be a true replacement for what a master could be to you—"

"No," she cuts in. "You'll be better because you're my friend."

I smile, thrilled she's happy about the arrangement rather than upset I didn't ask her first.

"Okay. Well, masters and their fledglings typically have a bond that solidifies when they spend the first months of their new lives together. It helps them to find each other should they need it. I know we can't have the same, but I wondered if you'd be open to something similar?"

Raine's eyes are a mix of confusion and enthusiasm. "How would we do that?"

I point to the shop just a little up the lane.

"Tattoos?!" she squeals. "Like matching ones? I mean, I don't get how that is the same, but I'm totally keen. Wait. Can vampires get tattoos? Can angels... uh, demons... um. Hybrids? Ugh, you know what I mean!"

I laugh, let go of her hands, and link my arm with hers, pulling her into a stroll. We bump into each other as our dresses dance together in time with our movements. A new lightness fills my heart as I soak up the joy that is my new friend walking by my side.

Thoroughly enjoying Raine's excitement over her new life, I add to it by leaning in and whispering, "Magical tattoos."

She jerks me to a halt, mouth popped open into a little *O* shape. "No way! Really?"

"Really," I promise. "They hurt." I nudge her and pull her back into a walk. "But probably not as much as the mind witch did."

She shivers. "Walk in the park, then, huh."

I push the door open, and we both look around in amazement. The walls are covered in tattoo stencils with all kinds of designs—symbols, animals, places—which are all changing colors or moving.

Raine squeals and runs over to a wall. "Oh my goodness. Did you see that? It just hid!"

I rush after her, curious. Sure enough, after a second, a panther slinks out from behind a tattoo stencil of a tree. "Wow!"

A mage wanders out from the back of the shop—a short guy wearing jeans, a T-shirt, and an easy smile. "How can I help?" he asks.

"Uh, we'd like to get something that matches."

Raine lets out a little squee of excitement, and a smile pulls up my cheeks so much it hurts. The guy looks amused as he watches us and waits patiently for our request.

"But we need something that will help us find each other when we're separated."

"Gotcha. Lemme get a sheet with options."

He rifles through some pages and brings one back to us.

"Any of these pairs will work or I can draw something up. They're all one of a kind anyway, and I don't make duplicates. Just so ya both know."

We hold the page together, a hand on each side. There's a mix of strange symbols that don't mean anything to me: building structures, vines, leaves.

"The rose!" we both say as we point at it together, then laugh.

The guy joins in with us, the joy infectious. "That is perfect. The roses only stay in bloom when you are close to each other. Otherwise, they return to buds. You can also use a word of power to activate a tracking function of sorts. It looks like this was meant to be, huh?"

I wink at Raine, and say to the mage, "You have no idea."

DID YOU ENJOY THIS BOOK?

Your feedback is so valuable to me as an author. If you enjoyed this story I would love for you to rate and review it on Goodreads, or on the paperback section of Amazon, or any social media platforms you use! Word of mouth is the best way for people to learn about stories they might enjoy.

ARE YOU DYING TO LEARN ABOUT EVERLEIGH'S FIRST CASE AS AN ENFORCER?

Good news! *Burned By Fury* is available for purchase on your local Amazon store and is also enrolled in Kindle Unlimited. Head there to get your copy today!

Meet The Author

SHAY LAURENT

Shay is a fantasy author who lives in south-western Sydney with her partner, three young princesses, and three pretty kitties. Aside from getting all the cuddles, her life mostly involves psychology, writing, and photography—not necessarily in that order.

Long before Shay started writing, she fell in love with all things fantasy. She thrives on escaping into the magic and mayhem of other authors, and spinning the tales that run wild in her mind in her own books.

If you want to keep up to date with Shay, head to https://linktr.ee/slauthor03where you can join *The Wolf Pack,* her reader group on Facebook, sign up to her newsletter on her website, or connect on socials.

Acknowledgements

THANK YOU

Thank you for taking the time to escape into *Haunted By Legacy*. I know each moment in our lives is precious and I'm grateful you decided to spend some of yours here. I hope you enjoyed reading this novella as much as I enjoyed crafting it.

Haunted By Legacy would not have come together without the support of some wonderful people, and I would love to take the time to thank them here.

Samantha Brennan—you are my writing rock! You keep me grounded and centred in the chaos that can be the life of an author. Your support on the tough days and encouragement on the good days make all the difference to me. I appreciate you more than you'll ever know, on and off the page.

To the team at Hot Tree Editing—you are all amazing! Donna, your kindness and professionalism made opening my inbox a delight. Kim, your final eyes read and comments made a huge difference to my confidence and reaffirmed that I was able to put together a story worth readying.

Becky, there aren't enough words! Your feedback on my story was everything I needed—warmth, encouragement, kindness, constructive—overall I know my novella and writing craft are improved because of your time and effort. I am eternally grateful!

My cover crew—Kristen, thank you for putting together a gorgeous cover that fit the vibe of my newest series! You were a true pleasure to work with. Your flexibility and kindness made all the difference, allowing me to soak up the joy that is putting a 'face' on my book baby. Julie, thanks so much for your time on creating the title graphics for this novella to make sure my wonderful readers could enjoy a consistent aesthetic across my Everleigh Cole novels.

Shannon and Rebecca—thank you both so much for beta reading my novella start to finish! This story wouldn't have made it to the level of quality it achieved without you both. Your warm words and constructive feedback kept me feeling motivated and encouraged to complete this prequel to my new series. I adored working with you both, and hope you enjoy the end result!

Finally, thank you to my partner, princesses, and kitties. You all give me the joy in life to *want* to write and share the stories in my mind. I love you all, always.